WART

ALSO BY ANNA MYERS

WART
Anna Myers

Walker & Company
New York

First published in the United States of America in 2007 by
Walker Publishing Company, Inc.
Distributed to the trade by Holtzbrinck Publishers

For information about permission to reproduce selections from
this book, write to Permissions, Walker & Company,
104 Fifth Avenue, New York, New York 10011

Library of Congress Cataloging-in-Publication Data
Myers, Anna.
Wart / Anna Myers.
p. cm.
Summary: A witch and her weird son may soon be joining Stewart's family,
but he would prefer his father marry the librarian he had been dating to
this new woman, even if the latter can make Stewart popular and improve
his basketball game through spells and charms.
ISBN-13: 978-0-8027-8977-8 • ISBN-10: 0-8027-8977-3 (hardcover)
[1. Single-parent families—Fiction. 2. Remarriage—Fiction.
3. Witchcraft—Fiction. 4. Popularity—Fiction. 5. Schools—Fiction.
6. Family life—Oklahoma—Fiction. 7. Oklahoma—Fiction.]
I. Title.
PZ7.M9814War 2007 [Fic]—dc22 2007006218

Visit Walker & Company's Web site at www.walkeryoungreaders.com

Book design by Nicole Gastonguay
Typeset by Westchester Book Composition
Printed in the U.S.A. by Quebecor World Fairfield
2 4 6 8 10 9 7 5 3 1

All papers used by Walker & Company are natural, recyclable products
made from wood grown in well-managed forests. The manufacturing processes
conform to the environmental regulations of the country of origin.

To William Charles Lane Jr.

This book is for you, Baby Will. I was writing it when you were born. We were wonderfully happy that day, but happiness turned to fear when we learned your tiny heart had four serious defects. Doctors told us, too, that your chromosomes were probably not normal. During your first nights at home, I sometimes sat up with you because your mommy and daddy were so worried about you that they woke each time you made a tiny sound. You and I would stay in the rocking chair together, and I would take you to your mother when you needed to eat. Those night hours were hard because I worried for you and for my own baby, your mother. However, they were sweet hours too. As we rocked together, I could feel the prayers being said for you by people in many places, some of them on the other side of the world. Those prayers were answered. The test telling us about your genetics took two weeks, but when it came back, it said your chromosomes were perfectly normal. When you were two months old, we made a long journey so that you could have a special doctor as your surgeon. We will always be grateful for Dr. Knott-Craig because he was able to repair your precious heart. You are four months old as I write this. You have the most expressive eyes I have ever seen on a baby, and you are always ready to smile and laugh. From your Grandmother Barbara you inherit the blood of Bluejacket, war chief of the Shawnees, from your mother's great-grandfather the blood of a pioneer teacher, and from your grandfather, who is in heaven, you receive the gentle spirit of a poet. I know you will grow into a man who would have made all of those before you proud. Welcome to the world, darling Will. You are a gift from God to us all.

Nana

WART

What Happened First

Stewart Wright wanted to be popular. It was a gradual, growing desire. It started the summer before eighth grade. It started with a visit from his cousin Sammi, who was sixteen and very pretty. It started at breakfast over strawberry pancakes. It started with a question, "Are you popular, Stew?" The rest of the family—Stewart's dad, his little sister, Georgia, Aunt Susan, Uncle David, and his little cousin Isabella—were all eating in the kitchen. Stewart and Sammi had carried their breakfast out to the sunroom, where Sammi asked the question.

Stewart wished they had stayed in the kitchen. In the kitchen, Sammi would not have asked the question. What could he say? His mouth was full. Good, he could chew for a long time. He did not look at Sammi. He looked out at the backyard, but he could feel Sammi looking at him.

She did not wait for him to stop chewing. "You aren't, are you?"

Stewart felt miserable. He had never cared about being popular before, oh maybe for a minute during class elections or when he heard some other guy talking about a party that Stewart had not been invited to attend, but the desire had been fleeting. Now, though, he suddenly understood. If Sammi thought being popular was important, it must be important. Stewart liked to impress Sammi, but he was not popular, not at all.

He shook his head, but he did not have to say anything. Sammi had plenty to say. "You know what? It's okay." She pushed her plate back on the wicker coffee table. "I can help you!" She got up and walked to the other side of the table where Stewart sat. Sammi put a hand on his shoulder, and with her other hand she turned his chin up, so that she could see his face. "I've been thinking about your problem ever since I got here."

Stewart frowned. He hadn't realized he had a problem, hadn't known that all last week, as he watched movies with Sammi or as they swam at Holden Lake, she had been troubled over his condition. Sammi gave his cheek a little pat before she went back to her place on the wicker couch. "Here's the thing, Stew. You've got a lot of stuff going for you." She held up one finger. "First, you're good looking." She gave her head a decided nod. "You really are." She put up another finger. "And you're smart, not too smart, not nerdy smart or anything, just right, really." She added a third finger. "And you're funny. I mean, you make me laugh all the time." She stopped talk-ing and looked at him.

Stewart knew she was waiting for him to say some-thing. He squirmed for a second, then realized what she expected from him. "So?" he asked. "What's wrong with me?"

Sammi leaned back against the flowered cushions. She folded her arms and nodded her head slowly several times. "It's your friends," she said. "Yes, I'm sure of it. You need new friends."

A feeling of panic started in Stewart's stomach and spread quickly. Stewart loved Sammi. Stewart wanted to please Sammi, had always wanted to please Sammi. But his friends? Sammi would fly back to California, and he would be left in Oklahoma. He would not see Sammi again until Christmas. She wanted him to have new friends? He shifted his weight. "Why?"

"Well," said Sammi. "Let's start with Ham." She closed her eyes for a second and drew in a deep breath. "There's his name. Nobody is named Ham."

"His name is Andrew Hamilton," said Stewart softly. "Ham is just a nickname. His family doesn't call him Ham or the teachers, either, very often."

"Well, sure, but the kids at school do, don't they?"

"Mostly. I guess."

"Well, then . . . ," Sammi was nodding her head again, "he's skinny, too, way skinny. Maybe the skinniest kid I've ever seen."

"He eats all the time."

Sammi put up her hand in a sort of stop gesture. "I know. Believe me, I've noticed, but that's not the point. Being that skinny isn't...." She paused and twisted her face, thinking. "Skinny is just not in, Stew, not for a boy anyway." She made a face. "He has no butt. Surely you've noticed! None at all! He's like that man on the TV show, the cartoon that's not for little kids where the guy tried to get a prosthesis, you know, a fake butt?"

"Huh?" Stewart shook his head. "There's such a thing?"

"It's a cartoon show, a joke, Stew. That's the thing, a person that skinny is funny, not popular, and ...," her voice got louder, "he's slow thinking isn't he? I mean the boy just isn't very sharp."

Stewart leaned toward her. Here was a point he could defend. "Ham does okay in school. He even got an A in math last year."

Sammi made a little disgusted sound with her breath. "I never said he was dumb. I said he isn't sharp. There's a difference, Stew. Don't you know that?"

Stewart did not know the difference, but he didn't say so. "Ham's been my best friend always."

"I know. I know, and I'm not saying be unkind to him." She spoke slowly as if trying to explain a difficult math problem. "Just put a little distance between yourself and the boy. I guarantee he can't be helping your position, popularity-wise, I mean. Face it, Stew, the boy is more of a pet than a friend."

It was true! Suddenly Stewart saw Ham through Sammi's eyes. Didn't he, Stewart, have all the ideas? Wasn't he the leader, always? Why had he never noticed? He might as well have carried peanuts to feed Ham or thrown balls for Ham to fetch.

Sammi turned her head briefly to the left toward Rachel's house, and the sick feeling in Stewart's stomach got even worse. Sammi was about to start on his next-door neighbor. "And that girl," she said, tilting her head in Rachel's direction.

"What's wrong with Rachel?" Stewart had trouble getting the words out. He knew some of what Sammi was about to say. Even he wasn't that out of things. Rachel *was* one of those nerdy smart kids. Everyone thought so. She could, Stewart was certain, rattle off the circumference of the earth, and he had watched her solve mammoth math problems in her head. Rachel knew all the presidents in order, too, but that was okay because Stewart himself was interested in the presidents and history. There was something wrong with the way Rachel dressed too. Stewart couldn't have explained exactly what, but he was vaguely aware that she didn't look like the other girls.

"What's wrong with Rachel?" Sammi repeated his question. She rolled her eyes. "Please, Stewart, do I really have to tell you?"

"Mom loved Rachel," Stewart said. It was true and the best defense he could have come up with. Stewart felt proud to have thought of it. His mother had been killed in a car accident almost five years ago, and he did not think about her so often, at least not every minute anymore. Sammi was the daughter of his mother's twin sister, and she, like her own mother, had loved Stewart's mother fiercely.

For a long minute Sammi said nothing. Then she sighed. "I'm not saying she isn't nice, and she was a really cute little girl. I remember how the two of you used to play Winnie the Pooh and Tigger." Sammi reached over to muss the hair on Stewart's head. "You were always Pooh, and she was always Tigger." She put out her hands toward Stewart and moved her fingers in a sort of calling motion. "Come on, Stew, you aren't in kindergarten anymore. Rachel has no figure, she has no style, she doesn't even have enough good common sense to care. You cannot, I repeat, cannot afford to be seen with her at school."

The popularity conversation had taken place on July 4. Sammi went home with her parents the next day. "Don't worry, Stew," she said when she hugged him good-bye, "I'm not deserting you. I'll e-mail you."

Stewart nodded, but he didn't smile. He was not fond of e-mails, sent none except to Sammi, and that only occasionally. He did not talk often on the phone either. Stewart Wright was not a communicator. He liked to play video games. He liked to watch movies. He liked to read, especially about history. Maybe he would just ignore Sammi's e-mails, but as he watched her walk away from him to get on the airplane with her parents, Stewart felt uneasy. Sammi had started something. She had made Stewart think about changing his life, and he was afraid he couldn't go backward.

When school was about to begin, Sammi bombarded him with e-mails. "What are you planning to wear?" she wanted to know. "Don't make any decisions until you run them by me." She insisted Stewart sign up for Instant Messaging even after he explained that he hardly ever went online. "You will be, Cuz," she said. "You're going to have lots of new friends this year. You just need to make a few changes in your life."

Stewart finally got up the nerve to tell Sammi he wanted to drop the whole thing, but Sammi wouldn't let him. "Okay, Stew," she wrote. "I'm not going to keep pushing, but I think you *do* want to be popular. I could feel it when we talked about it. Am I right? Hey, just let me know when you decide to take the right steps."

Stewart sat in front of his computer, his elbows on the desk. He lowered his head and rested his face in his hands. What would it feel like to be popular? Why not give Sammi's ideas a try? He sighed, but he didn't write back that he was ready. He did nothing to change his life either. At least he did nothing until the last week of October.

· ONE ·

What Happened Next

Later, Stewart Wright would wonder if there had been any sign, any warning, of what was to come. When he was ready for bed that October night, could he have gone to his window, pushed back the curtain, and looked up to see strange circles around the moon? If he had stayed awake instead of pulling the green and blue comforter up to his neck and sleeping immediately, would he have heard an odd wind blow up suddenly to whistle around the house, knock over garbage cans, and shake bright leaves from the trees?

The truth is that there was no real sign. From his yellow two-story home with white shutters on Eighth Street, Stewart would have observed no warning. However, had he been across town on Bell Street at just the right moment, that short slot of time when it is no longer day but not quite dark, he might have seen a sleek black car turn into a driveway in front of a stone house, a place that had stood empty for a long time now. Just the day before the front windows had been covered by overgrown shrubs. No one had noticed workmen coming into the yard to cut the bushes and trim the hedge. Yet what had once been out of control was now well manicured.

Had Stewart been there on Bell Street, he might have seen a woman step from that car and heard her say to a boy in the backseat, "Wake up, Ozgood. We have arrived at last." He might have noticed that the woman took no luggage from the car. Nor did she carry boxes as newcomers frequently do when they first move to a home.

From outside the windows of that stone house, Stewart would have seen that no one was inside before the woman and boy came, but strangely, a welcoming fire blazed in the fireplace and reflected the shine on tables and bookcases. Had he been near the door when the woman and the boy opened it, smells would have drifted from the kitchen, wonderful smells of roasting meat and baking cookies. He might have heard the woman say, "Ah, all is ready, just as I ordered."

But Stewart was not across town on Bell Street. He spent the time before he went to bed playing a game on his computer when he should have been doing his algebra assignment.

Because there was no warning, Stewart Wright slept well in his yellow house. In the morning, he woke when his dad knocked at his door and called, "Time to get up," but he wanted to go back to sleep, wanted to continue the funny dream. He had been in a race with other boys from his class, but the unusual thing was that Ham's grandmother was in the race too. In the dream, she was a great runner, and she and Stewart were leading all the others, even Brad Wilson. Then the knock came.

Stewart sat up and rubbed his eyes. Well, he thought, it didn't seem likely that Mrs. Hamilton, a gray-haired lady who sometimes used a cane, could win a race, but his own winning, that was a dream for sure. He wished he hadn't signed up for gym. Now that he was in eighth grade, it wasn't the old required PE class. Now they had basketball teams and played real games, but it was late October, way past the deadline for changing classes. Besides, his father wouldn't have agreed to his dropping out anyway. "Finish what you begin." He could hear his dad's voice in his head.

Then that same voice called from down the hall. "Stew, are you up?"

"Yes." He threw his legs off the bed and began to dress. The day started as usual, breakfast with his dad and little sister. Georgia was still excited every morning about going to kindergarten. Stewart ate his cereal and thought about how he had liked school back in elementary days, hadn't really hated it the first two years of middle school either. Only this year had it become almost unbearable. Two things made it horrible. He was not good at basketball, and he couldn't quit wondering about

< 10 >

being popular. Okay, he confessed to himself, there are three. He also couldn't stop thinking about Taylor Montgomery either.

His dad always drove Georgia to school on his way to teach at the college. She was in the dining room gathering her school things, but Stewart could still hear her chattering. Georgia was like their mother, a woman she couldn't even remember, always talking and at ease with people. Stewart looked at the family picture above the fireplace. Dad was holding baby Georgia, and there he was standing beside his mother, his arm around her shoulder. Life was so easy then.

Stewart got his books. On top of the stack was algebra. He frowned, remembering that he hadn't finished last night's homework. With a sigh he shoved the books into his backpack. Oh, well, there was no more hope for his algebra grade than there was for his athletic ability or popularity. For a minute he stood still, thinking. Sometimes he could hear his cousin's voice in his head. "You need new friends."

Stewart shrugged and went outside to sit on the front step and wait for Ham to come from his house around the corner, but outside the air was definitely cooler than yesterday. He went back for a jacket. When he came out again, Ham was standing on the sidewalk, and he was grinning. "Morning, Stew." Ham slapped him on the shoulder, and Stewart grunted a greeting. Sometimes Ham's good moods got on Stewart's nerves. Sometimes

Ham got on his nerves! Sometimes he wanted to walk away from Ham, just long enough to know if Sammi was right. Would he really be more popular without his old buddy?

Ham took a breakfast bar from his jacket pocket and began to unwrap it. "Didn't finish my breakfast." He pointed with the bar toward the house next door. "You want to see if Rach is ready to go?"

Stewart shook his head. "Nah, let her find her own way to school."

"Not exactly Mr. Sunshine this morning, are you?" Ham talked around the breakfast bar.

"Don't see what there is to be sunny about?"

"Cheer up," said Ham. He dusted the crumbs from the front of his jacket. "Things could be worse."

"Yeah, you think so?" Stewart slung his backpack over his shoulder and began to walk. "Just watch, and they probably will get worse."

"You know," said Ham, "this might be a really good day. Maybe today will be the day Harrison shows the video in art. I would have taken band if I hadn't heard about that video, all those naked women right there in class. He's supposed to show it during the first nine weeks, and time is running out."

"I've told you, they can't be pictures of naked women. Harrison couldn't get by with that. Probably just statues or something."

"Well, as long as they're naked, anyway. Even statues

would be better than nothing. I'm telling you, today is the day. I can't wait until art class."

They didn't talk much more on the way to school. The crisp autumn breeze touched their faces. Yellow mums filled flower beds and Halloween decorations hung in windows. Stewart wished he could forget about Taylor, who would never notice him. He wished he could stop caring about being a good basketball player. He wished he could quit having the urge to yell at Ham, who finished one breakfast bar and pulled another from his jacket pocket.

Their school, an old sandstone building that had once been the high school, covered almost a whole block. It was, Stewart thought, not really part of the town, not part of anything around it. Sequoyah Middle School was a kingdom, a kingdom ruled by the popular kids, a kingdom where Stewart had no real place. They climbed the big front steps and went inside. Stewart walked slightly ahead of Ham. No one noticed them. They separated to go to their classes.

When they met at the art room door third period, Ham poked Stewart. "Hey, look! He's pulled the video screen down. Didn't I tell you this was going to be the day?" Ham looked around the room. "Wonder where Harrison is? He's always in here when we come in." They made their way to a front table.

Stewart got interested when Taylor Montgomery took a seat at the end of their table. Lately, he had taken to watching Taylor all the time. It had started a few weeks earlier, when Stewart had walked behind Taylor in the hall. Her shiny blond hair had hung down below her shoulders, and it had bounced as she walked. Her body had bounced, too, and Stewart had followed her into a classroom before he realized that he should have stopped in the room before that one.

Stewart felt desperate. He wanted Taylor to notice him. He even e-mailed Sammi, "She's very popular. Any hints about how to get her to like me?"

Sammi wrote back a long answer all about how Stewart was such a great guy and how any girl would be lucky to have him for a boyfriend. She said Stewart should just be himself, but then came the part that made him uncomfortable. "You are staying away from Ham and Rachel, aren't you? You are never going to be part of the popular crowd if you're hanging around them." Stewart hadn't written back yet.

He was lost in thinking about Taylor and hardly noticed when the bell rang. Ham jabbed him in the ribs. "Maybe Mr. Harrison isn't here today," Ham said. "That's okay. Subs like to show videos."

Stewart didn't say anything. He went back to concentrating on watching Taylor without being obvious about it. Taylor was talking to her friend Madison. There was too much noise in the room for Stewart to hear what the girls said, but Taylor made a wonderful star in a silent movie. Stewart could watch all day.

Then Taylor stood up. "Hey, you guys!" she shouted. "We should be quiet and working when someone comes in. You know Mr. Dooley has been on a rampage lately. I don't want detention. I'm getting the charcoals."

As Stewart would have predicted, the room quieted down. People paid attention to Taylor. She was, after all, the most popular girl in the whole eighth grade. Until recently, Stewart hadn't thought much about such things, but until recently, he hadn't noticed how a girl's behind swayed when she walked either. Things were different now.

Stewart watched Taylor move to the supply closet and open the door. He heard her scream, and taking his eyes off her jeans, he saw what she was screaming about. What a sight! There was Mr. Harrison on the third shelf, right between the yarn and the bottles of glue. He gave Taylor a strange little wave.

Everyone got up and went over to the closet to get a better look. "Hey, Mr. Harrison," someone yelled. "What are you doing?" Mr. Harrison did not answer.

Instead, he took a ball of yellow yarn, unrolled a long piece, and began to weave it into his reddish beard.

"I think he's flipped," said Taylor, and she sounded like she was about to cry.

Stewart considered pushing his way to her side. He could take her hand and promise to take care of her. He didn't move.

"Mr. Harrison," called Ham, "can I have the bathroom pass?"

Stewart gave Ham a jab with his elbow. "Not now, dopey!"

"But I got to go real bad." Ham turned to look at the door, and Stewart knew he was considering leaving the room. He didn't, though, because the principal, Mr. Dooley, was coming through the door. He was moving pretty fast, and Coach Knox was behind him; so was Ashley Sage.

"See!" Ashley pointed toward the closet. "I told you so."

"Why'd Ashley go and ruin the fun?" Ham whispered, but Stewart didn't say anything. Coach Knox had come to stand right beside him, and the coach always made Stewart nervous.

Kids moved out of the way, and Mr. Dooley and Coach Knox stepped up close to the closet. "There is some explanation for this, right?" Mr. Dooley's face was red, and his bald head was starting to shine. "An experiment, right?"

Mr. Harrison didn't say anything, but he started to hum. Stewart was pretty sure it was the school song.

"Get down at once, Harrison!" Mr. Dooley pounded one fist into the other hand. Stewart expected to see steam coming out of his ears. "This constitutes flagrant neglect of duties, grounds for dismissal." He folded his arms across his chest and looked up at Mr. Harrison, who continued to hum, loudly now. Everyone could hear plainly that it was the school song, and Stewart had the urge to sing along. He didn't.

"Let me get him for you." Coach Knox rubbed his hands together in anticipation.

"Not in front of them," Mr. Dooley said in a sort of half whisper. He turned to the students and made a motion with his arm toward the door. "Go to the library. Go very quietly and take something to study."

They went, but not quietly. "Boy," said Ham when they were in the hall, "some teacher is always threatening to go bonkers, but I never thought I'd get to see one do it."

"Wow!" Stewart shook his head. "Do you think Coach will jerk him down by the leg, or will Mr. Dooley help and lift him down between them?"

"Wish we knew. I'm going to stop at the bathroom. You go on up and make sure we get the old *National Geographic* magazines. You know, the ones with the women with no clothes on top."

At lunch the cafeteria buzzed with talk about Mr. Harrison. Rachel almost always brought her lunch and was already eating an apple when Stew and Ham got through the line. "I feel bad for him," she said when they asked if she had heard about what happened.

Ham waved his hand in a motion of dismissal. "You feel worse because you missed it."

"Well," she said with a smile, "I guess it would have been kind of interesting."

"He might still be there if Ashley hadn't gone for Dooley," said Stewart, "but don't say anything Ham because here she comes." Ashley Sage was Rachel's only real friend besides Ham and Stewart, and the four almost always ate together. While Ashley settled herself, Stewart looked around.

The most popular kids sat in the middle of the cafeteria. Taylor Montgomery was always somewhere near the center. Today Brad Wilson and Jake Phillips were at the table with Taylor and her friends. That was becoming a pattern. One of the boys must have a thing for Taylor, maybe both of them. Brad and Jake were both the athletic type.

Stewart wondered what type he was. He glanced at the faces of the kids at his table. I'm the loser type, he told himself, and so are these others. He wondered about Sammi's comment. Would he be with the popular kids if it weren't for his friends? Would having Taylor like him make giving up Ham and Rachel worth it?

Right after lunch, Mr. Dooley came on the intercom. Usually kids yawned during Mr. Dooley's frequent intercom announcements. He didn't have much to say to individual students, but he did love to address the student body on the intercom. This time, though, they were interested. "Young ladies and gentleman," he began. "I know you are all concerned about our Mr. Harrison. Let me assure you he is being well cared for. Because his illness may keep him from us for some time, we are so lucky to have had a qualified teacher come to our building just today seeking a job. We are pleased to welcome Mrs. Wanda Gibbs who is an experienced art teacher. She will be with us covering Mr. Harrison's duties, including Open House tonight."

Stewart lowered his head and rested it in his hands. Open House! Suddenly Mr. Harrison's breakdown seemed like nothing to be interested in. He was facing a death sentence. Open House! He had forgotten about it, but he was pretty sure his father hadn't. It would be right there on the kitchen calendar, and his dad was sure to have noticed it. The algebra grade was bound to come up. Stewart had to find a way to keep his father home.

While his geography teacher talked about Europe and pointed to countries on the map, Stewart rolled his pencil between his hands and thought. Before the bell rang, he had a plan. Georgia! His little sister could be a real mess, but the two of them got along pretty well. If Stewart worked it right, he could get his little sister to do pretty much anything he wanted her to do. He would figure out a way to get Georgia to keep Dad from talking to Mr. Payne about his algebra grade.

At home, Stewart stood on the small front porch of the yellow house for a minute before going in. His father did not have a late class on Thursday afternoon and was already home. Mrs. Davis, called Gran by the kids, had already picked up Georgia from school as usual, and Stewart could smell the roast she had put in the oven before she left. "We'll have an early supper," Dad said right off. "Remember we go to your school tonight."

Stewart's heart sank. There went any hope he had that

his father might have forgotten. "It's no big deal." He went to the cabinet to get out glasses for the meal. "If you're tired, we can just stay home."

His father looked closely at him. "I wouldn't miss it."

Stewart decided it would be best not to push the not-going idea. He would just have to count on Georgia. "Guess what happened today in school," he said while they ate, but even as he told the story about Mr. Harrison, he was planning what he would say to his little sister.

After they ate, Stewart helped clean the kitchen, then went upstairs. Georgia was in her room playing with the little plastic horses she loved. Stewart dropped to the floor across from her. "Listen, Georgy," he said, "you've got to help me at my school tonight." He glanced at the door, making sure his father wasn't near. "When we are ready to go to the math room, I'll say, 'Algebra is next.' That's when you pitch a fit to go home." He put his hands on her shoulders and got his face close to hers. "This is really important. Life and Death. Don't let Dad go into that math room. Do whatever you have to do!"

Georgia looked up, her face twisted, deep in thought. Stewart knew she was pretending to consider the situation, but he was certain she would do it, would enjoy the challenge of it. "Okay," she finally said, and Stewart gave one of her pigtails a friendly tug.

On the way to school, Stewart made himself not think about algebra. He thought about the basketball team. The coach would be announcing this week who would make the real team, the one that competed against other schools. He wondered if he had any chance. With a sigh, he shook his head. Not likely.

Inside, Stewart guided his father and sister to English class first because it was first period, and because he liked taking his father to Miss Oliver first. "Stewart is a fine student. You must be very proud of him," she said to his father. Stewart looked down and resisted the urge to ask Miss Oliver if she didn't agree that in this age of super calculators math was pretty much unnecessary. Algebra wasn't until fifth period, but Stewart decided to get it over with.

They walked out of the English room, and Stewart said, "Let's go on to algebra now." He gave Georgia a meaningful look. She nodded slightly, but did nothing. Stewart stopped moving. "Algebra is just next door," he said forcefully.

They could see into the room. Mr. Payne was busy talking to one set of parents with another mother waiting.

"We could come back later," Stewart said, and he hoped he had kept his voice light. His father was forgetful. If they got away this time, he might not think of coming back.

"We're in no hurry." Dad stepped toward the door.

Stewart turned to Georgia. "Now," he mouthed.

"I want to go home," she whined, and she pulled at her father's jacket. "I'm tired and my tummy hurts."

Mr. Wright put his finger up to his lips to shush her. "In a few minutes."

"Now!" She was louder this time, and some people turned to look at the family.

"Be quiet," their father said with a determined tone.

Stewart stepped behind his father and gave his little sister a big smile and a thumbs-up sign. She threw herself on the floor and started to kick and scream. "Take me home to my little bed. I'm tired and so sick. Take me home, oh please, Daddy! Take me home." Everyone in the hall was staring now, and some people stepped out from rooms to see what was going on.

"Stop it!" Dad leaned down and jerked on Georgia's arm. Stewart was afraid she would straighten up like she usually did when their father really showed she had gone too far.

"Let me talk to her." He leaned down. "Stop acting like a little brat," he said, but all the while he smiled.

She let out an even louder wail. "I think she might be really sick," said Stewart, who was beginning to feel a little guilty for getting his little sister in trouble.

That's when it happened. That's the moment Stewart's life began to change. Suddenly there was a woman in front of them. Stewart had just time enough to notice her unusual looks. Her hair was black as the darkest night, and it hung in a big long braid down her back. The really different thing, though, were her eyes. They were the brightest green eyes he'd ever seen. Without a word to anyone else, she bent over and looked into Georgia's face. "What's the matter, sweetheart?" She put one hand under Georgia's chin. The other hand was touching a big green piece of jewelry hanging from a gold chain around her neck.

"Nothing," said Georgia in a sweet, little voice. Stewart wanted to pass out.

"I'm Wanda Gibbs," the woman said, turning to their father. "I'm the art teacher." Substitute, Stewart wanted to yell. After all, poor Mr. Harrison was just crazy, not dead. He might come back.

"How nice to meet you," Mr. Wright said, and Stewart wanted to throw up. Here was this nosy woman butting in where she wasn't wanted, and Dad was practically kissing her feet. What was even worse, Georgia was holding her hand and smiling at the woman like a perfect angel.

"Come on down to my room, darling. I'm not getting many parents." She was patting Georgia's cheek now, but her other hand was still on that green necklace. "You can color some pictures while your daddy visits with Mr. Payne." She gave Stewart's father another big smile, and Stewart thought Dad nodded in a sort of dopey way.

Then they were gone, the woman leading Georgia by the hand. His little sister didn't even look back. "How nice of Wanda," Mr. Wright said, like they were old friends. Then he turned and went into the math room.

Just as Stewart expected, his father got pretty worked up over the algebra grade. "No more TV," he said when they were in the hall again. "No more computer, no more iPod." By the time they had gone through the other classes, he had calmed down. "Okay, Stewart," he said. "I do want you to spend less time watching TV and playing games, but I'm also going to help you. We're going to work on algebra together regularly. You're too smart to make low grades."

Stewart felt better that he didn't have to lie to his dad about his algebra trouble anymore, but they had saved the art room for last, and on the way, he started to worry about what his dad was going to do if he found out Georgia's fit had been his idea. "I need to go to the restroom," he said when they were just outside the door. "You can go on in and get Georgia if you want."

He did go down the hall to the restroom and came back to wait outside the art room, trying to think what to do if his dad came out mad. The amazing thing was that his father and Georgia both came out wearing big smiles.

On the way to the car, Stewart decided to be quiet and hope for the best, but what his father said after he had started the car surprised Stewart into forgetting to worry about punishment. "I asked Wanda Gibbs to go out to dinner with me tomorrow evening," he said.

"Oh!" Georgia clapped her hands. "She might be my new mommy!"

Stewart gave the little rat the dirtiest look possible. It was too dark, though, and the look was wasted. Not only had Georgia let him down, now she was being disloyal to their mother and to Martha too.

· TWO ·

It felt strange the next day to sit in class and be taught by the woman his dad was going to take out to dinner. He and Ham stared at her as she talked. Then Ham wrote a note. "Why?" He scribbled in the margin of the paper where he had started to take notes about perspective. Stewart shrugged his shoulders. "She's not near as pretty as Martha," Ham added. Stewart shrugged his shoulders again.

Then Stewart quit even pretending to pay attention and started to think about Martha. He sure hoped she didn't call while his dad and Ms. Gibbs were gone. He didn't want to be the one to tell her about the date, and Martha might ask where his father was.

He sighed. Sure he had told his dad right out that he didn't like the idea of his getting married again. Still, he had always liked Martha. He didn't want a stepmother.

That was all, and his dad didn't seem to be in any hurry to remarry either. Dad was like that, taking things very slowly. Martha was nice and patient, never pushing his father beyond an occasional dinner and a play. Stewart couldn't even remember how many years they had been sort of dating. He had always figured that some day his father would want a woman in their family, and he had thought that woman would be Martha.

Why would his dad suddenly want to date Ms. Gibbs? She was a short woman and definitely on the pudgy side. Stewart reached for Ham's paper and added his own note. "I'd say Gobbs might be a better name for her than Gibbs. Have you had a look at her behind?"

He poked Ham, expecting him to look down at the paper and then grin. Ham didn't respond at all.

A cold chill came over Stewart, and he knew even before he saw the hand with the long red fingernails. Slowly he turned his head, and for just a split second before he looked down, he stared into those bright green eyes. "Give me the note," she said. Stewart laid it in her hand.

The room was deadly silent. Ms. Gibbs took the note, read it, folded it carefully, and tucked it into the pocket of her sweater. Then she walked to the board, took a marker, and said, "I need to write myself a little reminder." In big letters she wrote STEWART. She stepped back for a second as if to examine the word. "Do you have a nickname?" She turned to look at Stewart as she asked the question.

"Kind of, well . . . sometimes." Stewart's voice sounded shaky in his own ears.

"Is it Stew?" She turned back to the board, picked up an eraser, and took off the first three letters. "Or it could be Wart, couldn't it?" She whirled back to stare at Stewart. She moved to allow her gaze to take in all the kids, and she smiled. "Time will tell, won't it, class?"

The class laughed, and for just a second, Stewart thought even Ham was going to smile. "Now," said Ms. Gibbs, "back to perspective." Stewart was glad the period was almost over.

In the hall, he leaned against the first locker he came to. "I'm dead," he said to Ham. "Did you see the look she gave me, and then that Wart business. She's out to get me."

Ham pulled at his arm. "Ah, I don't know. She could have sent us both to the office. Dooley wouldn't be very easy on us for giving her trouble. He wouldn't want her to leave him with Harrison the way he is. Cheer up. It's lunchtime."

The cafeteria always had the same smell no matter what the meal was. Stewart stood behind Ham in line and wondered about the odor. In front of Ham stood Brad Wilson, king of the eighth grade. Stewart glanced in Brad's direction, but Brad didn't turn toward them until after Jake Phillips came to stand behind Stewart. "Hey, Jake," Brad called. "I saw Coach in the hall just now, and he told me he's giving out the basketball uniforms today."

Stewart did not even hear Jake's reply. What a blow! He would be humiliated today in the gym just like he had been humiliated in art class. There were only twelve basketball uniforms and twenty-six boys in the class. Twelve would be given uniforms and allowed to play in an after-school league, against other schools! The other fourteen boys would be divided into two teams that would play each other. Stewart wanted to be one of the twelve. He wanted it desperately!

Stewart looked at Ham, who had a weak little smile on his face. Well, they both knew Ham had a chance, a small chance, but at least a chance. They didn't talk much during lunch. Ham had the good sense not to tell Stewart to cheer up, and he was glad to eat the French fries Stewart pushed toward him.

During geography, Stewart tried not to think about basketball, tried not to think about how great it would be to be on the real team. He liked the game, but it was more than that. He bit at his lip. If he could be a good player, he would be popular. He was sure of it. At Christmas he could tell Sammi. He wouldn't say anything at first. He would wait till maybe the second day they were together. Then he would say, "Oh, by the way, I am popular now." He would shrug and pretend it was no big deal. "Yeah," he would add, "I guess it sort of started after I made the team."

Between geography and science, Ham came to Stewart's locker. "You eat that candy bar you had in there yesterday?" he wanted to know. Stewart dug under a pile of books, found a mashed chocolate bar, and handed it to Ham without a word. "Don't look so worried," Ham said. "I think you're going to make the team." He unwrapped the candy bar and started to eat.

Stewart slammed his locker door. What made Ham so sure he was worried, and how could he be so skinny and stuff himself like that? "We'd better hurry. The bell's about to ring." He stomped away. Inside the science room, Stewart slumped down in his seat and waited, his eyes going constantly to the clock. Finally, the bell rang.

Ham didn't say anything on the way to the gym, and Stewart felt grateful for that. Coach told the boys to settle on the floor to wait. Stewart's heart was pounding so loud that he expected someone to say something about the noise. Brad Wilson was the first person to be called. That was no surprise. He got up and walked down to the dressing room to try on uniforms. The way he moved, so full of confidence, really got to Stewart. He considered taking one of his brand-new basketball shoes out of his gym bag and throwing it at Brad. At least that way the price of the shoes wouldn't be wasted.

Coach kept calling off names, Dave Stills, Jake Phillips, Carlos Valdez. Stewart was counting. Ham was too, putting out a finger each time the coach called a name. Two hands were almost used, only two fingers left. That meant four more names would be called. "Andrew Hamilton." Stewart felt proud of himself because he really was glad for his friend, and he managed to smile. "Matt Lawson, Obi Muonelo, Stewart Wright." Stewart couldn't believe it. At first, he thought about asking the coach if he had heard correctly, but instead he got up slowly. He wanted to walk off like he had been certain all along that he'd be included, but he couldn't. His walk was never right. Neither could he stop feeling bad for the other boys, the ones stuck on the reject teams.

Brad and Jake were already changed and standing on the dressing room steps when Stewart started down. "Hey congratulations, Wart," Brad said when Stewart passed them.

Oh great, the name was going to stick. If Brad Wilson used it, so would the rest of the school. Stewart forced a little grin and moved on. Then he heard Jake say, "Wart got lucky. Green and Russell were too fat for the last uniform."

"Yeah," said Brad. "If either of those guys had weighed ten pounds less, that Wart wouldn't have made the team."

Stewart tried not to let the comments take away his pleasure. Brad and Jake didn't know everything. You made it, he told himself. That's the miracle you wanted. Now just work hard and get your game improved. The coach let them wear their uniforms while they did dribbling drills. Feeling first-rate, Stewart put everything he had into the workout. He made a couple of layups, and didn't even mind when someone yelled, "Way to go, Wart." He was on the real team, part of the Rams.

When gym class ended, Stewart looked forward to a relaxing Friday evening alone. Georgia had taken her sleeping bag and gone straight from school to a sleep-over. His father would be out with Ms. Gibbs, which was pretty weird, but at least he would have the house to himself. He was pretty sure Dad wouldn't mention anything about not watching TV or playing games while he was gone.

Of course, the peaceful evening thing didn't work out. The first problem was Martha, who drove up just after Stewart got into the house. He saw her car from the front window just after he stepped inside. She got out of her blue Toyota and carried a paper bag toward the house. Maybe he should just go upstairs and ignore the doorbell, but she had probably seen him. Well, he just wouldn't mention his father's plans for the evening even if she came right out and asked. Why should he do Dad's dirty work? Let him tell Martha himself that he was taking out another woman.

"Dad's not here," Stewart said as soon as they had said hello at the door. He hoped she would leave right off, but she walked in and went to the kitchen with the bag. Stewart followed.

"Don't look so miserable, Stewart." She gave him a big smile. "I made pizza and had lots left over. I knew you would be eating alone tonight, so I brought some over to you."

Ordinarily the thought of Martha's homemade pizza

could make Stewart forget almost any problem, but this time it didn't help. Martha knew Dad was going out to-night, but her smile made it obvious that she didn't know he had a date.

"Wow, thanks." He didn't look at her.

"Stewart, I know your father has a date with Wanda." She put the pizza in the microwave.

"You do?"

"Yes, don't worry about me. Wanda is an old college friend of mine."

Stewart studied her face. Things were sure getting weird. No one was acting the way they were supposed to. "How come you don't mind? Don't you like Dad any-more?"

Her smile had just about turned into a laugh. "Let's just say things have a way of working out for the best. You never did like the idea of your father and me getting serious anyway."

Stewart couldn't deny that. He stood there confused, saying nothing.

"Eat your pizza, and don't distress yourself over your father's romantic life. Trust him. He's a strong, in-telligent man." With a wave she headed toward the door. Again Stewart followed. His father had just driven up, and he watched as he and Martha talked for just a minute in the yard.

They look right together, Stewart thought. He stepped back from the doorway. Why had he never been comfortable about his dad dating Martha? Well, Martha wasn't worried. Probably Dad would go out with Ms. Gibbs only once. Suddenly Stewart realized he was starving, and he went to the kitchen for pizza.

His father came in just before he was settled at the table to eat. "Stew," he said right off. "I talked to Wanda on the way home, and I told her you would stay with her son tonight while we go out."

"Her son?" Stewart almost dropped his pizza.

"He's eight years old. They are new in town and don't have a regular sitter."

"Rachel." Stewart motioned with his head toward the house next door. "You know Rach does lots of babysitting."

"You're doing some tonight." There was an edge to his father's voice. Then he sort of grinned, sorry he had come on so strong. "Well, Ozgood is kind of shy. You don't mind doing me a special favor, do you?"

"Ozgood?"

"So he has a strange name. Give the kid a chance. You might like him. Anyway, I need this favor. Wanda asked for you. Said she was sure she could trust you." His father looked straight at Stewart, waiting.

"Okay." Stewart knew his father didn't ask for much from him. Besides he couldn't afford to cross Ms. Gibbs. She still had his note. How bad could it be? He'd take his Game Boy.

Worse than Stewart could ever have imagined! That's

how bad it was. Ozgood met them at the door. At lea. that's what Stewart finally figured out. At first, he thought it was just this giant pair of glasses. Then he discovered that there really was a boy wearing them.

"I'm Ozgood V. Gibbs," the glasses said, and a small hand was held out to them. "I do not care to be called Ozzy. I was named for the Wizard of Oz, who, by the way, was very real, as were his magic powers."

Stewart's dad took the hand and shook it. Stewart only stared. Then *she* came down the stairs, and he had something else to stare at. No one could have convinced him that pudgy Ms. Gibbs could ever have looked so good. She had on a white dress that was all soft and flowing looking. There wasn't anything plump about her, but it was her face that was really something. It was absolutely beautiful, and her eyes danced brightly. Stewart noticed that she still wore the same green stone around her neck. Suddenly a phrase came to Stewart's mind: The bride looked radiant. He gave his head a shake to get rid of the words. He wondered whatever made him think of such a thing. His dad let out a quiet whistle. It's like a magic spell, Stewart thought.

Ms. Gibbs and his dad were talking softly to each other. Stewart sank down on the stairs. His stomach felt strange, and he had the definite feeling that life as he had known it was over.

"Have a nice evening with Stewart," Ms. Gibbs said to Ozgood." She turned to Stewart. "Of course you won't

but there are some emergency numbers by
I don't carry a cell, but I'm sure you know
's number. I just wrote down some others to
anything you want from the fridge." She gave
him a little wave, and they were gone.

"If you don't mind, I believe I will now retire to my room to enjoy some music." Ozgood pushed up his glasses and started to climb the stairs.

"Wait." Stewart was failing as a babysitter. He did not want Ms. Gibbs to be mad at him. He waved the Game Boy. "Don't you want to play a game?"

"No. Thank you. I do not care for games."

Well, let the little weirdo go to his room. He'd just find the TV and some food. There wasn't one in the living room or the kitchen. He opened a door into what he thought might be some kind of family room, but it was completely empty. The TVs must be in the bedrooms. It was a good thing he had his own entertainment.

Then the music started. It was horrible, the kind of stuff from the old movies where a monster or maniac is sneaking up on the hero or heroine. And it was loud, so loud it seemed to bounce off the walls.

"Turn it down!" Stewart yelled, but he could hardly hear his own voice. At the top of the stairs, it wasn't hard to tell which of the three rooms was Ozgood's.

Stewart pushed open the door. The room was dark, but the light switch was right near the door. When light flooded everywhere, Stewart let out a whistle. This was no normal kid's room. On the wall was a huge picture of Dracula. In one corner was a big white table full of bones. The curtains and bedspread were black and red. Ozgood was in the bed, propped up on one elbow, staring at Stewart.

"Turn it down," Stewart yelled again. His eyes fell on the iHome. Why didn't the kid use the earphones?

Ozgood only stared at him. Stewart was ready to choke the kid when finally Ozgood leaned out of bed toward the iHome. After he tuned it down, he turned back toward Stewart. "I'm sorry. You will need to repeat what you were saying to me."

"I was yelling to turn it down." Stewart eased down on a chair beside the door. The room was fascinating. He wanted to look around without getting far from the escape hatch.

"You would probably prefer some foolish band." Ozgood leaned back on his pillow.

"Well, yeah, but not so loud. The neighbors will call the police." Stewart wanted to go over to look at the bones. Could he tell if they were human?

Ozgood followed Stewart's gaze. "I'm a serious science student," he said.

"Sure." It was all Stewart could think of to say. Then he looked at the poster. "That's neat." He pointed at Dracula.

"I rather enjoy the story." Ozgood snuggled down on his pillow. "But it isn't true, you know."

"Sure." Stewart's vocabulary was starting to seem pretty small. He'd go downstairs and find some way to amuse himself. He got up and moved toward the door.

"They will be married," Ozgood said.

"Who?" Stewart turned back to look at him.

"Our parents, of course." He had a worried look on his face.

Poor kid, Stewart thought. He didn't understand at all. "Oh no." He wanted to reassure him. "They just went out to eat. Seafood, Dad said. They'll be back before you know it."

"But," Ozgood let out a long sigh. "They will be married. She says he is Mr. Right."

That one made Stewart laugh. "It's just our name, Wright. Look, lots of women have wanted to marry my dad, but he has a mind of his own. If he wanted to get married, he'd already be married." Stewart turned back toward the door.

"Is he a match for a witch?"

Stewart stopped, walked back, and sat down again on the chair. "What are you talking about?" The kid obviously wanted to get his attention. Maybe the boy was lonely.

"I asked if your father is a match for a witch because my mother is one." He wasn't smiling.

"Ozgood, that is not a good thing to say. Your mother is very nice." Actually, Stewart wasn't crazy about Ms. Gibbs, but "witch" did seem a little strong.

"No!" Ozgood rolled over to face the wall. "I am trying to warn you despite great peril to myself. My mother is a true witch. She will use her spells on your father, and if she learns that I have told you the truth, she will turn me into a frog."

Stewart laughed out loud. "Your mirth will be short-lived," Ozgood said.

The kid was more than lonely. He was nuts! Stewart got up and walked again to the door. "You'd better get some sleep now." He went out and closed the door. What a kid. He couldn't wait to tell Ham. He'd go downstairs and call him right away.

He had seen a phone in the kitchen. Stewart wished for the first time that he had a cell phone. Lots of kids he knew had them, but he had never particularly wanted one. He had no one to call except Ham. The home phone worked fine for that. When he went somewhere, Ham was pretty likely to be with him, so a cell phone had never seemed necessary. He wondered if Ms. Gibbs might have some kind of recording thing on her phone. Oh well, he'd chance it.

All the way to the kitchen, Stewart turned often to look over his shoulder, expecting Ozgood to sneak up behind him. He didn't think the whole thing was funny. His father was out with a woman who had a nutcase for a son.

On a pad beside the phone was the note, "In case of emergency, call Martha Long." Martha's number was written there too. Stewart shook his head. This whole deal was about as weird as it could get. It seemed Martha was practically giving Dad to Ms. Gibbs. He leaned against a wall and dialed Ham, who answered right off. "Everything over here is really wild."

"Yeah? How?" Ham was munching something that sounded like chips.

It all came tumbling out. "Ms. Gibbs looks real good, drop-dead gorgeous even! And the kid! His room's all done in black and red with bones and Dracula." Ham tried to say something, but Stewart went on talking. "But listen. I haven't told you the big thing yet. He claims she is a witch! Ozgood said it, and he might be a frog. Martha says don't worry, but I'm worried plenty!"

"I didn't get all that," said Ham. "Hold on. I need some dip."

While Ham was gone, Stewart took long deep breaths, and he felt calmer when Ham picked up the phone again. "The main thing is," he told Ham, "this kid is real strange. You wouldn't believe how he talks, like some old school teacher. He plays creepy music and has bones in his room."

"Really?"

"Yeah. But the big thing is that he claims his mother is a witch who plans to use a spell to make my father marry her."

"Wow! What are you going to do?"

"Well, there isn't a TV. Guess I'll just hang around,

play on my Game Boy, and wait for Dad to come back."

"No." Ham sounded aggravated. "I mean what are you planning to do about the witch and your dad?"

"Ham!" It was Stewart's turn to be aggravated. "You don't believe that stuff?"

"Well, I don't know." There was a pause while he chewed. "You know something, I think I kind of do. There's something about that woman."

A sort of chill came over Stewart. "I better go check on the kid," he said, and he hung up the phone.

No sound came from Ozgood's room. Stewart wandered back down the stairs and stretched out on the couch. Determined not to think about Wanda the witch and her little warlock, he decided to daydream about Taylor Montgomery. In the dream he needed her to be about to marry some dismal fellow. Oh, Brad Wilson would work. He was down on Brad after the Wart thing and the comment about why he made the team. Anyway, he was pretty sure Brad really did like Taylor too. All the boys did. Okay, Brad is a miserable bag boy at a grocery store. It isn't clear why Taylor is about to marry him, but she is until tragedy strikes. Taylor comes down with a terrible brain tumor, and no one thinks surgery can save her. Stewart, who is the top brain surgeon in the world is called in to operate.

Brad gets all teary eyed and begs Stewart to forgive him for the Wart calling. He also begs Stewart not to charge much because being a bag boy does not pay much.

Just before Taylor is put under, Stewart takes her head in his hands and looks long into her beautiful blue eyes. "Stewart," she murmurs, "I know now that I always loved you." They kiss and then he performs this miraculous surgery. All the female nurses get down on their knees and kiss Stewart's hand. Taylor recovers. Stewart and Taylor get married, and he arranges with the grocery store owner to make Brad an inside stock boy, which is a real step up.

He was just at the place where Taylor's hair was growing back when he heard the car. Dad and Ms. Gibbs were home. He jumped up because his feet were on the couch. Then he stood there, all nervous, while they came in.

"We're back," Dad announced when they stepped inside, and Stewart was shocked to see that they were holding hands.

Stewart, anxious to get all the good-byes and thank-yous said, edged toward the door. When they were in the car, he unloaded on his father. "That Ozgood is a real space cadet." He slumped down in the seat, leaned back, and closed his eyes.

"Interested in space, huh?" Dad obviously wasn't really listening.

"No," Stewart sat up and made his voice very distinct. "I mean he is out in space, loony, not in touch with reality."

"Wanda mentioned that he is going through a sort of hard time." Dad was fiddling with the radio.

"Hard time!" Stewart was practically yelling. "He claims his mother is a witch."

"Really?" This wasn't like Dad. He always paid attention when Stewart was serious. "You know, son, you could be a big help to a boy like that, a sort of . . ." He paused for a minute. "A sort of big brother."

Stewart slid back down on the seat and closed his eyes, but he certainly did not sleep. He had to think, had to plan. Man! He had never wanted Dad to get serious about Martha, good old regular librarian Martha. At this point he would dance at his father's wedding if he would marry Martha. He had to do something to stop this romance. Now!

They were almost home before Stewart found the strength to talk again. "Dad, doesn't it bother Martha at all, you taking out Ms. Gibbs?"

They were turning into the driveway. "No," said Dad. "Martha is such a sensible woman. Says she always knew things wouldn't work out between us because you kids didn't want me to get serious."

"I like Martha." His voice sounded desperate. "So does Georgy." Boy did he like Martha. "Dad," he said, "I was wrong to complain about you and Martha. You have your life to lead."

His father stopped the car. "I'm glad you feel that way, Stew, because I am going to tell you straight out. There is something special about Wanda. Something I can't quite put into words, but I haven't felt this way for a very long time."

His father got out then, but Stewart sat still until his

dad called him. He felt too tired to open the door and was amazed that he could actually climb the stairs. He went straight to bed. All night he dreamed about Dracula and frogs.

The next day he felt better. Probably, he told himself, he had gotten all worked up over nothing. It was a pretty regular day at first. Dad went after Georgia about midmorning, but instead of coming into the house, she went next door, where Rachel sat on her front porch playing with the puppies. Rachel's Dalmatian, Molly Dot, had four puppies. Molly Dot was not an ordinary dog. Rachel had taught her all sorts of tricks and was hoping Molly Dot would win a talent show a big pet store was holding the day after Thanksgiving. The audience would hold little voting machines. Rachel planned to have Georgia hold one of the puppies up front while Molly Dot performed because that might appeal to the audience.

Stewart could see Rachel's front porch from his window, and he decided to join the girls. Dad had promised Georgia he would buy one of the puppies, called Little Dots by Rachel, for her birthday in early December. Stewart and Georgia spent lots of time trying to decide which Dot she wanted.

"I like this one best, maybe. Look, I think he's got more dots," said Georgia, and she held up a squirming black-and-white puppy. The puppies had been born white, getting their spots only as they got a little older.

"Let's don't decide until they're a little bigger," said Stewart, and he took the warm little body from his sister's hands. "This one is nice, though, but maybe we ought to see them run first."

"Dalmatians aren't racing dogs," said Rachel. "What difference does it make how they run? They aren't greyhounds."

Stewart didn't answer. Sometimes Rachel got on his nerves. Why did he have to live next door to her all his life? Wouldn't it have been wonderful to live next to Taylor Montgomery?

After a while, Ham came from around the corner. He carried a basketball under his arm. "Want to shoot some baskets?" he asked Stewart. The boys went back to Stewart's driveway to use the hoop up over the garage door.

Ham wasn't great, but Stewart was terrible. Only two of his first fifteen shots went into the basket. He felt sweaty and nervous. He had to get better.

Rachel left Georgia with the puppies and came over to stand near where the boys played. "Stewart," she said, "why do you break your neck trying so hard at basketball? Do you really like it that much? I mean, you don't have to be an athlete."

"Yes, Rachel, I like it that much." Stewart aimed the ball at the hoop, but he considered throwing it at Rachel.

"Okay, Wart," she said. "I just wondered."

"Don't call me that, Rachel Thomas. Don't you ever call me that again!"

"Boy, are you getting touchy." Rachel went back to the puppies.

Stewart was glad when his father called them for lunch. At least he was glad until the announcement. Stewart had finished one tuna sandwich and was reaching for another, when his father said, "Wanda has invited us all over for dinner tonight." Suddenly, Stewart couldn't eat another sandwich. He carried his dishes to the dishwasher, then went upstairs to wait for Georgia. He would try his little sister one more time. When he heard her on the stairs, he went to the door to motion her toward his room.

He led her into his room, closed the door, and pointed her toward the desk chair. He sat on the edge of his bed that was near her. "Listen," he told her. "Dad is getting pretty serious about that woman, and she's got the creepiest little kid you can imagine. His name is Ozgood." Stewart twisted his face. "Isn't that a disgusting name? If Dad marries Ms. Gibbs, that little fart will be our brother. You won't get anything you want ever again. You will be just like Cinderella. 'Bring me my breakfast in bed,' Ozgood will say, and you will run up with it. 'Pick up my dirty socks,' he will yell, and you will run to get them. Your little legs will be so tired." Stewart looked down at Georgia and saw a tiny tear on her cheek. Encouraged, he went on. "Dad will be too busy with his new son's problems to notice either of us. And of course there won't be any money for new little ponies or dolls because Ozgood eats an awful lot and probably has to go to a head doctor every Thursday."

Georgia jumped from her chair. "What can we do to stop Daddy from getting a marriage?" Her lips pressed together, ready for a fight.

"Scream," he said. "Refuse to go to her house. Say you want Martha for a new mommy. Say you are afraid of Ms. Gibbs." Stewart was beginning to be pleased with himself. He would not just sit and watch while his father ruined all their lives.

"But you always told me we didn't want a new mommy at all," said Georgia.

"Well," said Stewart. "That was before Wanda Gibbs came to town on her broom. Now Martha seems pretty good."

Stewart sent Georgia down the stairs, and he waited at the top, just out of sight, but close enough to hear. She didn't go right into the screaming. The kid is really smart, Stewart thought. "Daddy," she said real soft. "Can we just stay home tonight? I'm feeling awful sad inside."

Stewart could imagine his Dad putting down his paper to look at Georgia. "Why baby?" he said. "Why do you feel sad?"

"I'm afraid you like Ms. Gibbs better than me," she said.

Oh, that's good, Stewart thought, and he smiled. The kid has really got it. "Of course, not," Dad said. Stewart inched down the stairs so that he could see what was going on. Georgia sat on the floor leaning against Dad's leg as he sat in his favorite chair. Dad was patting her head. "You and Stewart are the most important people in my life, always."

"Can we just stay home tonight then? You and us important people and fix some popcorn and watch a movie? Please, Daddy."

"Well." He was weakening. Stewart could hear it in his voice. "I wonder if Wanda has started to cook yet."

"Call her, Daddy. Tell her your little girl needs you." Georgia sounded like she might start to cry.

Dad stood up and started for the phone, but just then the doorbell rang. Stewart's hopes took a nosedive when he saw Ms. Gibbs. "I was in the neighborhood," she explained, "when I got this idea that Georgia might want to come on to my house early and help me fix dinner." She was smiling, and Stewart saw his little sister inching closer to the woman.

Stewart ran down the stairs and grabbed Georgia by the arm. "You were going to help me with that special project, remember?" He gave her a threatening look and a little jerk toward him.

"Oh yeah. I forgot." She didn't sound too sure, but she looked up at Ms. Gibbs. "Besides Daddy was going to call—"

"Wait, now, Georgia," Dad interrupted her. "Helping Wanda cook dinner might be a lot of fun."

Ms. Gibbs dropped down to her knees. She was wearing her same necklace, and she started to finger it as she talked. "Actually, I'm sort of lonely." She was looking right into Georgia's eyes. "My little boy stays in his room so much. I could use a little girl for company."

"Oh!" Georgia clapped her hands. " I love to be company!" Georgia was jumping up and down.

"But Georgia, what about helping me, remember?" Stewart squeezed her arm, but she pulled away.

"I'll help you later, Stew," she said.

Before Stewart could think what to do, they were heading toward the door. "Open the door for Wanda and your sister," his father called.

Wanda brushed against Stewart's shoulder as she went out. "Thank you, Wart," she said softly.

· THREE ·

Stewart and his father spent a few hours working on algebra. It felt good to be working with Dad. Stewart remembered what Martha had said about how he should trust his father. She had called Dad a strong, intelligent man. Surely Dad wouldn't get too involved with the Gibbses. Stewart felt pretty good until they were on their way across town to Ms. Gibbs's house.

Dad was half singing and half humming. Stewart didn't know the name of the song, but every once in a while he caught the word *love*, which made him very uncomfortable. Stewart hunched beside his door and stayed absolutely quiet.

Ms. Gibbs and the little traitor met them at the door. Georgia was just as pleased with herself as she could be. "Wanda let me put things in! Salt and cheese and everything." Stewart got the picture of his little sister and a witch in black clothing stirring a big black cauldron like the ones in Halloween posters. The witch had Ms. Gibbs's face. Stop that, he told himself.

His dad got really close to Ms. Gibbs to say hello. For one terrible minute Stewart thought his father was going to kiss her right there in front of everyone. His expression must have been pretty sour because Ms. Gibbs came over and touched his shoulder.

Her green eyes were dancing, and she gave the boy a wide smile. "Cheer up, Stewart. You look like a prisoner about to have his last meal."

He felt that way too. Feed me, he thought, then finish me off. Ozgood came in just as they were about to sit down and took a chair beside Stewart. "I am undone," he whispered. Stewart looked down at his pants, but they were zipped just fine. Then he remembered "undone" was an old way of saying a person was in a real trouble.

When Stewart saw the food, though, he forgot about Ozgood and all his other problems for a minute. It was wonderful—lasagna, tiny green peas with onions, a great salad, and hot bread that smelled heavenly. Stewart's mouth was watering until his father said, "Lasagna! How did you know that's my favorite?"

Stewart's throat went dry, and all he wanted was water. "I made a lucky choice, didn't I?" Wanda said. She leaned toward James Wright and smiled sweetly, but as Stewart reached for his glass, he caught the look she threw at Ozgood. It wasn't a sweet smile.

Stewart gave himself a little talking to. Come on, he thought, forget it all and chow down. You don't get a chance at food like this very often. So he dug in. Sometimes, though, right in the middle of a wonderful mouthful, the phrase, *prisoner's last meal* would flash through his head. Still, he ate two helpings of everything.

When it was time for dessert, Ms. Gibbs brought in a big cherry pie. "Wow!" Dad had a huge grin on his face. "You must have magic powers. Cherry is my all-time favorite."

Ozgood let out a strained little cough and poked Stewart. "Ozgood," said his mother, do you need to leave the table?" This time Stewart was certain of the dirty look Ozgood's mother sent her son.

"I am recovered," Ozgood said, but when Ms. Gibbs's back was turned to serve the pie, he leaned close to Stewart. "Woe is me," he whispered. "She knows I have betrayed her."

Stewart wasn't sure if he wanted to laugh or cry. Here was this little wimp of a kid who said things like, "I am undone," and "Woe is me." It would have been hilarious except that he had this horrible feeling that his dad was going to get them all mixed up with the little fruitcake and his wacky mother. Wacky Wanda, he thought. Then he changed it to Wanda the Witch. Alliteration! His English teacher would have been proud of him. But even making up names for her didn't improve his mood. Oh, he wasn't really taking the witch business seriously, he told himself, but he knew Wanda and Ozgood were too weird for his straitlaced dad and his two motherless children. Boy, was he sorry he hadn't warmed up more to the idea of his father and Martha getting married.

After dinner, Stewart thought maybe they'd hang around for just a little while, then go home. Of course, it didn't work like that. "I think Wanda and I will go out for a while and hear some music. You kids could watch some TV or something," Dad said.

They were in the kitchen, everyone pitching in on the dishes. Stewart turned to his father, "I was hoping to get in some more algebra study." Stewart thought Dad would be impressed, but he just laughed. "Besides," he added, "there isn't a TV downstairs."

"Oh, I should have told you last night." Wanda was bent over to put away pots and pans. She straightened and looked at him. "There's a TV in the game room."

He left the kitchen and went to the room behind the dining room. The door was open, but he couldn't remember it being open when he'd been in the living room the night before. He stepped into what had been an empty room. The first thing he saw was a pool table at one end of the room. At the other end stood a cozy arrangement of a couch and two chairs, centered around a big-screen TV. It was one of those thin ones, and the screen was huge. This was crazy. This room had been totally empty last night. Why hadn't Ms. Gibbs just said the stuff had arrived today? A person would think she had just zapped it up.

"I never thought Mother would allow a television in her house. She hates some of the silly witch things they have on. Guess she wanted to go out rather fiercely." Ozgood stood in the doorway behind Stewart. "I've never seen one so large." He walked around Stewart and went over to examine it like he was seeing the thing for the first time. He picked up the remote and pushed a button. "There," he said triumphantly when it came on.

Georgia came in rubbing her eyes, tired from the sleepover the night before. "I'm just going to rest my eyes a little bit." She stretched out on the couch and was asleep immediately. Great, Stewart thought, he was headed for another evening alone with weirdo Ozgood.

It didn't take his dad and Wanda long to finish in the kitchen. Stewart could see that they seemed eager to dump the kids and be gone. "You guys have fun," Dad said, and Stewart grunted.

"Yes." Ms. Gibbs had her hand on Ozgood's shoulder, and she bent her head to look right into his face. "Have a good time, but follow the rules."

"She expects me to tell you that I made up the witch story," Ozgood said as soon as they heard the front door close. He began to pace the floor, his hands clasped behind his back. "I won't do it. There is my integrity to consider!" He dropped into a big chair. Sitting there with his face in his hands, he looked small and pitiful, but before Stewart could think of anything to say, Ozgood was up and walking again. "In all likelihood I shall be severely punished. Woe is me!" He paced out of the room.

He's not a bad actor, Stewart thought, and he walked over to make sure Georgia was asleep. He sure didn't want her to hear this crazy stuff. She already had bad dreams sometimes.

"I'm going up to await my fate," Ozgood called from the other room. Stewart got in there just in time to see him sort of dragging himself toward the stairs. His expression was so dejected that Stewart forgot he was acting and felt sorry for him, but the sympathy didn't last long because he put on that eardrum-splitting music right away. It sounded like a funeral with the volume turned way, way up.

It didn't take Stewart long to get up the stairs and to his room. He pounded on the door. Of course, Ozgood couldn't hear him, so Stewart pushed the door open. "Ozgood," he yelled, trying to be louder than the music. "Turn it down!" He was already crossing the room to shut the thing off himself when he realized the room was empty. He's hiding in the closet or under the bed, Stewart thought. Ha-ha! Big funny joke. Stewart was ready to find him and let him know he wasn't laughing.

He stopped the music and went for the closet door, ready to jump on the kid and drag him out. What he saw was not Ozgood. Still, Stewart jumped all right, practically out of his pants. He yelled too, two short squeals like a scared rabbit. There, hanging between the shirts and pants was a skeleton, and it sort of swayed toward him. "Serious science student," he reminded himself, when he could think again, and he dropped to the floor for a look under the bed. "Planned the whole thing, knew I'd look in the closet. Probably giggling over the scream," he muttered aloud.

But Ozgood wasn't under the bed. Stewart was getting really aggravated "Ozgood," he yelled. "Front and center! Move it! Now!" There was no response. Stewart looked around. It was a little room with no other hiding places.

By the time he got out to the hall his temper was really rising. "Ozgood has disappeared," he could imagine himself saying to Ms. Gibbs and his father when they came back. For all he knew Weird Wanda might be glad to be rid of the little dork, but Dad would definitely see the whole thing as an indication that he was just not a responsible individual. At this rate he wouldn't be allowed to drive or go to a concert until he was at least thirty. The baby isn't supposed to turn up missing when you babysit, even if the baby is an eight-year-old nutcase.

It was clear Stewart would have to search the upstairs. He looked at the doors that were not Ozgood's, drew in his breath, and headed toward one. It led to a small bathroom, no place to hide except the shower. Reaching for the curtain, his hand shook, but he jerked it back. His breath came out in heavy relief. After the skeleton, he expected something bloody, but all he saw were panty hose hanging there to dry.

Next, he went into Ms. Gibbs's room. The closet didn't have bones, and it didn't have Ozgood. He switched on a light to be sure. There were two big shelves on each closet wall, and they were full of bottles. The closet was full of mixed smells. Stewart shook his head. The woman must make perfume, but none of the smells appealed to him. The kid wasn't under the bed either. Frantically, he ran back to the hall.

It was then that he almost stepped on the frog. Probably he would have squashed it if it hadn't let out a really big croak and jumped out of his way. Stewart stopped short and stared at the thing. "Ha-ha," he said loudly and sarcastically. "Very good, Ozgood, you can come out now."

The frog made a little hop toward Ozgood's room. Stewart jumped over him, ran down the stairs, and searched frantically. He looked in the kitchen cabinets. In the little laundry room off the kitchen, he opened the dryer and the clothes hamper. Ozgood was not inside the house, but the front and back doors still had the inside lock turned.

Absolute panic threatened to overtake Stewart, and he began to shake. He had to have help. It seemed ridiculous to call Ham, who was the only person Stewart knew who was a bigger goof-up than himself. Still, he didn't know what else to do. He did not know the number for Frog Busters.

"Listen," he said when Ham answered. "You've got to get over here." Ham said that he could get a ride with his sister, who was about to leave the house anyway. Stewart told him where Ms. Gibbs lived. Then he had another idea. "Stop by Rachel's and get her. Don't tell her anything except that I need help with my algebra." Rachel was always trying to help him, but he didn't want to tell her right off why he wanted her to come. She would think it was some kind of joke and refuse to play along.

"Why do you want Rach? I thought you didn't much want her around anymore."

Stewart felt uncomfortable. So Ham had noticed. Stewart twisted his face, wondering if Ham had also picked up that sometimes Stewart wasn't really eager to be around him either. There was no time to dwell on the "popular" issue now, though. He thought for just a minute before he answered. "We might need a girl to kiss a frog and turn him back into a boy."

Ham drew in his breath. "She did it, huh? Ms. Gibbs turned her own son into a frog. That's big-time stuff!"

"It was a joke, Ham." Stewart wasn't certain he had sounded very sure. He added, "There are no such things as witches, not in real life."

Ham ignored what Stewart said. "Don't worry," he said. "I'll be right over there to help you."

Stewart wasn't about to stop worrying, but he did want company. "Hurry," he said and was ready to hang up, but Ham had a question.

"Is there anything over there to eat?"

"Sure, if you don't mind food cooked in a witch's cauldron."

"I'll bring my own snacks," said Ham before he put down the phone.

Sitting at the bottom of the stairs seemed like the best thing to do. First, though, he would go up to check on the frog. It was in Ozgood's room, jumping and croaking like it was upset. "You think you've got troubles?" Stewart said to it. "Wait till you see what my dad does to me."

Then a thought came to him. The windows! There must be a tree or maybe even a balcony. He raced around the bed and over to the only window in the room. Nothing was visible when he moved back the curtain, but he wanted to raise it to be sure. There were no locks. Leaning against the frame, he pushed up with all his might. Nothing budged, probably painted shut.

Leaving the frog, he dashed into Ms. Gibbs's room and then checked the bathroom. No windows would open. Slowly, he went back down the stairs and dropped, exhausted, onto the bottom one. He tried to daydream about Taylor. He couldn't get his mind on that, so he sat there sweating until the doorbell rang.

"Where's the poor little thing?" Ham asked when Stewart opened the door.

"What poor little thing?" Rachel stepped around Ham. "You were acting awful funny on the way over here." She turned to Stewart, her face all screwed up, making her freckles run together. It was the expression she got when she was about to get worked up. "What's the deal?" she demanded. Stewart sank back on the stairs. It just wasn't a story he could tell standing up.

Stewart was amazed at the way Rachel believed the witch thing right off. Oh, sure, Ham believed it, but that didn't shock Stewart much. Ham was no rocket scientist, but Rachel! Stewart expected her to be full of questions and skepticism.

"Is the frog male or female?" she asked when they had started to climb the stairs.

Stewart threw his arms up in exasperation. "How would I know if it's a boy or a girl? It wasn't wearing pink or blue booties."

"Well," she complained, waving her algebra book, "if you had told me the truth, I'd have brought a good biology book. The frog's sex is important because if it is a girl, it isn't Ozgood."

Stewart stopped climbing and stared at her. Ham stopped too, and he started to dig into the bag of chips he carried. "Look," Stewart said, trying to sound calm, "this frog stuff is just a joke. I got you two over here to help me search for the kid."

"Witches scare me," said Ham.

When they were outside Ozgood's door, Ham latched onto Stewart's shirt. "Let's just get out of this place," he said.

"Quiet," Stewart whispered. "The little fart can probably hear us. He's hiding somewhere, laughing his head off." He looked over his shoulder and to both sides.

Inside the room, they got down on their hands and knees around the frog. "Poor Ozzy," Ham said.

Stewart jabbed him in the ribs. "Don't call him that. He hates it." Stewart gave himself a little shake. "I mean Ozgood doesn't like the name. This is just a frog." Sweat was dripping from his forehead, as if he were in the middle of a fast-moving basketball game.

"Should I kiss him now, you think?" Rachel was puckering up her mouth.

"Yikes! You two actually believe this is Ozgood!" Stewart wiped at his forehead with his shirtsleeve.

They both looked at him. "You believe it too," said Rachel. "Only you're afraid to admit it."

Stewart put his head in his hands. "Well, would you want a frog for a stepbrother?" A little weak feeling was starting down in the pit of his stomach. Maybe he did believe it. There absolutely was no place for Ozgood to be hiding that he hadn't searched. Just then the frog gave a huge hop and landed on the bed.

"Oh," said Rachel, "the poor little thing wants to go to beddy-bye." She looked around the room. "Let's get his pajamas."

Digging in the top bureau drawer, Stewart found a pair, black with pictures of all the famous monsters in red. He let out a big groan, and he handed them to Rachel. It was so crazy. Rachel was a really smart girl, a genius maybe. How could such a sharp mind believe the frog was a kid named Ozgood who was going through a witch family's version of being grounded?

Rachel was making a sort of little nest of the pajamas,

and she put the frog in the center. "Are you going to kiss him good night?" Ham was down on his knees beside the bed, like he was trying to establish eye contact the way they had been told to do during the public speaking class at school.

"Well, sure I am." She bent and gave the frog a big, loud smack on the back. "Poor kid is probably scared to death."

Stewart sort of stumbled out of the room, leaving them to turn off the light. "Don't look for a teddy bear or anything," he said over his shoulder. "Ozgood wouldn't have one, but he might sleep with a favorite skull."

Pretty soon they came to join Stewart on the bottom stair. Rachel had a proud smile. "He seems to have fallen asleep," she said.

Ham put his hand on Stewart's shoulder. "Old buddy," he said, "your life sure isn't going to be dull with a witch for a stepmother."

Stewart jumped up. "Number one," he yelled with one finger in the air. "My dad isn't marrying Ms. Gibbs. Until a few days ago, he was happy dating Martha. And number two." He added another finger. "This is all some joke. Ozgood is a pretty smart little kid, but he is not," his voice got even louder, "I repeat, NOT a frog."

"Don't get excited," said Ham. "Let's find something to eat and just do some thinking.

They passed Ham's chip bag around several times while they brainstormed, but no one had any real ideas.

When they heard the car in the driveway, Stewart realized he had to come up with an explanation that covered why Rachel and Ham were with him.

"We decided to work on some algebra problems," he said when they came in, and he held up Rachel's book. "I hope you don't mind, me having company, I mean." He glanced at Ms. Gibbs, who was watching him with her eyes narrowed almost shut, looking, he thought, deep into his soul.

Then she smiled. "Certainly, Stewart. I want you to feel at home here. Were there any problems with Ozgood?"

Stewart stared down at his shoes. What should he say? He wondered what would happen if he came right out and said something about the little frog being settled down for the night, but before he could decide, there was a sound from the top of the stairs.

"Oh, you're home." It was Ozgood's voice. Stewart whirled around. Ozgood was standing there in the pajamas Stewart had taken from the drawer. "I think I'll just go back to bed now. Your friends are quite charming, Stewart, especially Rachel." He gave them a little wave, turned, and walked away. Then he stopped. "Mother, dear," he said without looking back. "I shall be on my best behavior henceforth."

"Sweet kid," said Rachel, looking like she was about to cry. Stewart shot her a dirty look and then gave the same frown to Ham. He didn't want either of them talking. He sank back down on the stairs, too weak legged to stand up. He could feel his father studying him.

"Stewart looks a little pale, must be exhausted. Maybe I'd better gather up Georgia and head for home," he said.

"Good." Stewart held onto the bannister and pulled himself up. "I really don't feel so good."

The good-byes were short because Dad was holding Georgia in his arms. In the car nobody said much. Stewart leaned back against the seat and tried to rest. They dropped Ham off at his house. Rachel unloaded at the Wrights to go next door. "Don't worry," she whispered to Stewart before the car stopped. "I'll help you."

He did worry, though. Stewart worried a lot. For a couple of hours he sat in the window seat and stared out into the night, wondering what was going to happen next. Finally he stumbled over to his bed and fell asleep, but when he woke the next morning, his first thought was Witch! She's a witch!

· FOUR ·

Sunday was a quiet day. Stewart stayed in his room a lot because he just couldn't handle looking at his father. He even did some extra algebra problems. He thought some about the first basketball game that was coming up on Tuesday after school. He wondered if he'd get to play or just warm the bench. Basketball had been so important to him once, but now he couldn't feel too concerned. Nothing mattered when he compared it to his father's involvement with the witch and her little warlock.

By Monday morning, Stewart's strength had begun to return. Even just a day removed from the outrageous events of Saturday night made them seem less true. Witches weren't real, were they? There had to be an explanation for the frog stunt, but whether Ms. Gibbs was a real witch or a very strange lady with a kid who wanted to drive him crazy wasn't the actual point. She had to be stopped from getting more involved with his father.

Stewart lay in bed awake before his alarm went off, and he tried to plan. Maybe he'd go to Mr. Dooley. "Look," he could say. "You've got to get rid of Ms. Gibbs. The woman is a witch who turns people into frogs." Oh sure, great idea. He'd probably end up in a straitjacket, maybe sharing a room with Mr. Harrison at the funny farm.

Maybe he should just go straight to Ms. Gibbs. He could slick his hair back, borrow a black leather jacket, and try to be a tough guy. "Me and my Dad," he could sort of snarl the words, "we ain't lookin' to get involved with no witches." He was enjoying the scene in his head, but suddenly he couldn't see himself standing there in the tough pose. Instead, he got a picture of a frog hopping out of the art room, trying to catch up with Ham.

Well, why should he be thinking of going to Mr. Dooley or facing Ms. Gibbs? He hadn't even tried talking to his own father, not really. It wouldn't be easy. Neither Stewart nor his father were communicators. Stewart knew for sure that his father loved him and that his father would always take care of him, but they didn't spend a lot of time talking, not about important things. There would have been lots more talking in the family if his mother hadn't been taken away from them, but still, Dad was a reasonable man. Stewart would talk to him. He had it. Just as Dad and Georgia started out for school, he'd ask to ride along, telling Dad there was something he wanted to discuss. Right after the alarm went off, he called Ham's house.

"Please tell Ham not to wait for me this morning," he told Mrs. Hamilton. "I've got to ride with my dad." Stewart felt pretty confident about his plan as he went downstairs to eat.

His father was in a great mood. "Sure," he said when Stewart said he wanted a ride so they could talk. On the drive their father kept pointing out pretty trees for Stewart and Georgia to look at. It was late October. The leaves were bright with color, but Stewart hardly noticed. He was planning what to say. This might be the most important speech of his life.

When Georgia jumped out at her school and waved at them, Stewart got his courage up. He wasn't doing this just for himself. He had a little sister to consider. They were pulling back onto the main street, when he started. "Dad, you've got to be careful!" The words came out faster and more excited than he'd meant for them to, sort of a scream.

Dad slammed his foot on the brake and threw his head from side to side looking for the car or body he supposed he was about to hit. "Stewart," it was Dad's turn to yell, and his face was red. "What the devil are you doing?"

It was not a good beginning, but Stewart swallowed hard and pushed on. "Sorry," he said. "I didn't mean driving, I meant with Ms. Gibbs. That's why you've got to be careful. She's . . . she's not normal like us. Ozgood got turned into a frog Saturday night, just hopping around and croaking all over the place."

His dad didn't say anything, but he pulled off the street and stopped under a huge maple tree. A red leaf drifted down on the windshield as they stopped. Stewart thought it would be a great place for a picnic, but he knew they weren't about to have one.

"Look, Stewart," his father talked slowly and calmly, and Stewart's hopes rose. Maybe Dad was going to be reasonable. "I know you don't want me to get involved with Wanda. You don't want me to marry anyone." He stopped for a minute and looked at Stewart, who knew his father wasn't finished and that he should keep his mouth shut. "I can understand that, son. I know it's hard for you to think I'm replacing your mother. What I can't understand is your making up crazy stories in an effort to stop me. We've always been straight with each other, haven't we?"

Stewart bit at his lip. "Dad, it's true. She's a witch. Ask Ham and Rachel."

Dad reached over and put his hand on Stewart's shoulder. "Give it some time, Stew. We've got time."

"Probably not much," Stewart looked down at the floor. He knew there was no use saying anything else.

Dad started the car again, and neither of them said anything more until he stopped in front of the school.

Stewart opened the door. "You know," said his father, "you need a mother and so does Georgia. Maybe some- day Wanda could be a big help to all of us."

Stewart sighed and closed the car door after him. Help? Sure. She could zap him up a Porsche when he learned to drive. Of course by then he'd probably be a per- manent member of the frog kingdom. Frogs don't need sports cars.

He sat through his first two classes in a sort of daze, noticing nothing until Taylor got up to go to the pencil sharpener. Even then he watched her swinging hips as if he were in some dream instead of real life, but he was wide awake when he walked into the art room.

Ms. Gibbs was waiting at the door. "May I speak to you, Stewart?" She smiled sweetly at him. He felt cold all over, but with his eyes down he followed her to the corner of the classroom and stood beside her desk. "Don't fight me, dear," she said in a half whisper. "You can't win, Wart. Besides you should give me a chance to show you what I can do for you."

"Do for me?" He looked down at the floor. She had her hand on that strange green necklace, and Stewart was afraid to meet her eyes.

"Yes," she said, "for instance, I know you like Taylor Montgomery. A woman could give you little tips and things about how to impress girls. I know too that you love basketball. Who knows, I might even be a help with your game."

"How?" Let her believe she's convincing me, he thought.

"Oh," she touched his shoulder, "let's just say I have my ways."

"Ms. Gibbs," someone yelled. "I spilled paint." She turned away to look, and Stewart escaped to his place at the table beside Ham.

"What'd she say?" Ham whispered.

"Says she can help me with Taylor and basketball." Stewart kept his eyes on Ms. Gibbs while she cleaned up the paint. "I'm going to play along with her. Get proof. You know, beat her at her own game."

"Man," said Ham. "That will be hard to do. You haven't had a bit of experience turning people into frogs."

At lunch, Ham and Stewart headed toward a table where Rachel sat at one end by herself. Stewart put down his tray. "I hope no one bothers us," he said.

Rachel rolled her eyes. "Ashley won't be here all week. She's going to Alaska to see her brother. No one else is likely to sit down. It's not exactly like the whole world is dying to eat with us."

"We've got to get a plan." Stewart had been repeating those words to himself over and over. He knew there was a desperate sound to his voice as he said them aloud. Ham had begun to spread mustard on his hamburger and didn't even look up, but Stewart could see that Rachel was about to say something.

"Halloween is coming up real soon," she said slowly, still thinking as she formed the words. "Witches are supposed to do special things on Halloween." As she talked she waved her spoon back and forth. Rachel frequently ate her dessert first, and the spoon had chocolate pudding on it, but Stewart didn't even care if the stuff flew off and hit him in the face. If moving her spoon helped Rachel think, he could take some goop in his face.

"Yeah. Yeah." He urged her on by using his hands like he would to call a dog to him. "Keep thinking. What else?"

"Well, if she thinks you've warmed up to her, maybe she would be off guard. We might catch her at something."

"Take pictures or stuff for proof." Stewart leaned across the table, resting his elbows as close to Rachel as he could get.

"No, wait." Ham pointed to his mouth and the others waited while he swallowed his bite of hamburger. "I read in this book that witches can't have their pictures taken. They don't show up on film or something."

"I think that's just made-up stuff, you know, for books." Rachel went back to eating her pudding.

"Well," Ham said, and Stewart could see that his feelings were hurt. "How do we know the business about witches doing junk on Halloween isn't just made up for books too?"

"That's good thinking, Ham," Stewart nodded. He couldn't afford to let either of them get discouraged with helping him. They weren't much, but they were all he had. "But still I think Rachel's idea is worth a try."

"Halloween is Friday night. We don't have much time to plan our strategy," said Rachel. "We're going to have to go over there."

To show how short their time really was, the first bell rang, which meant they had to scarf down their last bites and put up the trays. Stewart saw Rachel in the hall before last period. "Wait for me after school," she said. "I've got something to tell you." There was an excited tone in her voice. He wanted to ask her what was up, but she hurried on to her class. Stewart did not go after her. He couldn't chance being late to gym class.

After school, Ham and Stewart stood out front until finally Rachel came out. "What took you so long?" Stewart asked.

Rachel put her hands on her hips. "If I had a friend who was trying to save me from a witch, I wouldn't complain about having to wait for her for a few minutes." She started to walk, and the boys fell in on either side of her.

"Sorry," said Stewart. "You sounded like you were on to something, and I'm anxious to hear about it, that's all."

"I think I am on to something." Rachel's expression was full of satisfaction and so was the nod of her head. Stewart waited, but she didn't say anything else. He chewed on his lower lip.

"What? What? Spill it!" said Ham.

Rachel stopped walking, drew in a deep breath, and said, "Well, I asked myself, where could we turn for help, and, of course, I knew the answer—the Internet. You can find anything on the Internet. When I got my English assignment finished early, I asked to go to the library. You know how they have the computers fixed so what you look up is limited? Well, I was pretty sure I couldn't use those computers to look up witches, so I just went to Mrs. Reynolds and I told her right out that I wanted to read about witches, and she didn't even ask me why, just said I could use her computer."

"Sure the librarian is going to like you when you've read practically every book in the library," said Ham.

Rachel went on "Well, let me tell you when you put in witches, you get all sorts of stuff. Mostly these people want to charge you for spells or potions to make you attract love or money or success or something."

"I don't have much money." Stewart tried to remember how much cash he had in his top bureau drawer. "Maybe fifteen dollars."

"Not enough." Rachel shook her head. "Even the cheap spells cost nineteen ninety-nine."

"I could chip in," said Ham.

"No," said Rachel. "The thing is, I'm pretty sure those things aren't real. I'm pretty sure real witches wouldn't have a Web site and be willing to take Visa cards. Why would they? A real witch wouldn't need to make money that way, now would she?"

"So, did Ms. Gibbs have a Web site?" asked Stewart.

"She did not. I kept on looking. Finally I got to things people had posted, free stuff, about spells and how to undo them. I was just about to write some things down when I realized the bell was about to ring, so I went back after school." She reached around to get her backpack and pulled out a sheet of paper. "I had to take notes because I couldn't print that stuff. You know how they have to approve anything you print, and I thought I might be pushing Mrs. Reynolds too much if I asked to print it."

Stewart reached for the paper, but Rachel held it away from him. "You couldn't read my writing. I wrote down what seemed like the best thing we could do. We have to get several onions and some garlic, chop it all up and mix it together. Then we divide it up into small portions and stick them in corners of the house. A witch will have no power in a house protected by onions and garlic."

"Oh, I don't know." Stewart's shoulders slumped. "That doesn't make much sense to me."

"Wouldn't it be awful smelly?" said Ham.

"No, listen, the article said the stuff could be wrapped up tight, you know in foil or something. Regular people don't have to be able to smell it, but a witch can. We can even hide it under rugs and stuff. I read a testimonial by this woman who claimed she had a friend, and she didn't know her friend was a witch until the woman went running out of her house after she did the onion and garlic thing."

Stewart shook his head. "So if she didn't suspect her friend was a witch, why did she put the junk around her house in the first place?"

"She was having bad luck. She thought it was caused by her husband's sister, but it turned out she was blaming the wrong person." Rachel put the paper back in her backpack and started to walk. "Of course, it's up to you, Stew, but if I thought my dad was about to marry a witch, I would try just about anything."

There was a supermarket just a block off their way home. Stewart shrugged. "Okay," he said, "we'll go to the store. How much money do you two have? I'll pay you back."

"I've got a five-dollar bill," said Ham. "Are onions and garlic expensive?"

"Who knows? I hope not because I've only got fifty cents," said Stewart.

"I don't have any money with me, but I can go home and get some if I have to." Rachel smiled at Stewart. "We're going to help you, just like I said."

More money wasn't necessary. With five dollars they were able to buy four onions and a whole pound of garlic. Ham even got a little change. "We're in luck on one thing," Stewart told the others after they had paid and were on their way home. "Dad told me this morning that Gran isn't staying today after she brings Georgia home. She's just going to make sure I'm home before she leaves. We can go to work right away. Do we have to cook the stuff?"

Rachel stopped to read the paper in her hand. "No, it says here, 'Place chopped onion and garlic together, wrap in foil, and place in corners of all rooms in which a witch or warlock is thought to be casting spells. Protection will be provided as long as material has not decayed.'" She shook her head. "There's not a word about cooking. Oh, I forgot about this other story. A woman named Margaret says a witch she worked with wanted the promotion Margaret had been promised. For a while it looked like the boss was leaning toward the witch, but after Margaret did the onion thing, the witch turned in her resignation."

"Sounds bogus to me," said Stewart as they entered the kitchen, "but it's all we've got right now."

They had just spread the onions on the countertop when Georgia came bouncing in. Stewart hurried out the front door to talk to Gran, so that she wouldn't come in.

Back in the kitchen, Ham and Rachel had the wooden chopping board full of onions. "I guess I ought to do the cutting up. I mean it is my life we're trying to save."

"We'll all have a turn," said Rachel. "We're in this with you."

Ham had chopped most of the onions when the doorbell rang. "I'll get it," Georgia called from the family room, where she was watching TV.

"Wait," Stewart headed toward the front of the house. "You know you aren't supposed to go to the door by yourself."

"It's okay," called Georgia. "It's just Wanda. I can see her through the window."

"No," Stewart yelled. "Stop! Don't let her in," but he could already hear Ms. Gibbs's voice saying hello to his little sister. He whirled to look back through the kitchen door. There was Ham, knife in hand, standing beside Rachel who held garlic.

Before Stewart could say anything, Ms. Gibbs was beside him. "Stewart," she said, peering around him into the kitchen, "how nice that you have your friends here." She stepped around him and into the kitchen. "Hello Rachel, Andrew, whatever are you doing?" She reached out to touch an onion that lay unsliced beside the chopping board.

"It's for supper," Ham said. "We're helping Stew get ready for supper."

"Gran already made supper." Georgia had come into the kitchen behind Ms. Gibbs. "She made a chicken pot-pie." She pointed toward the refrigerator. "It's in there. Remember, she told you to put it in the oven at five?"

"Oh yeah," said Stewart, and he knew his voice sounded shaky. "That's right. I kind of forgot, and we were making . . . soup. Onion soup, it's one of my favorites."

"Such a lot of onions and garlic too," said Ms. Gibbs. "I think you may have overdone it slightly. I can't think of any recipe that would call for that much of either ingredient."

"We . . . ah," Stewart tried to say something, but gave up.

"I hope you didn't get a recipe off the Internet. You know you can't trust what you find there. I even read a bunch of nonsense there once about how to stop a witch's powers by using onions and garlic." Ms. Gibbs laughed. "Isn't that ridiculous?" She laughed again. "So foolish, believing in witchcraft! I mean this is the twenty-first century." She turned back then to the family room and took Georgia by the hand. "Come along, dear," she said. "I want to measure you because I am going to make you a new dress." She took a measuring tape from her purse. Stewart stepped just inside the room, but he didn't go far from Ham and Rachel, who stood in the doorway between the rooms.

"Oh yes," said Georgia. She grinned and clapped her hands. "I love new dresses. What will it look like?"

"It will be a very special dress." Ms. Gibbs dropped to her knees and put the tape around Georgia's waist. "A dress so special you could wear it to be a flower girl in a wedding. Doesn't that sound nice?"

Georgia squealed. "What color will it be?"

"Oh," said Ms. Gibbs. "I don't think the color scheme has been decided yet for the wedding. Do you have any suggestions?"

"Pink," said Georgia. "I love pink."

Stewart swallowed hard. "Black," he turned toward the kitchen and mouthed the word to Ham and Rachel.

Ms. Gibbs measured from Georgia's waist to the floor, took a pad and pen from her handbag, and wrote down some numbers. "I must fly away now." She laughed. "Of course, I don't mean that literally, but I do have to go. Ozgood's lesson is almost over, and I must pick him up." She rose and moved toward the door.

"What kind of lessons does Ozgood take?" asked Rachel.

Ms. Gibbs turned back slightly and smiled. "Well, aren't you sweet to be interested in a little boy's lessons? I could tell the other night that you and Ozgood had made a rather special connection. He is at the aquarium. Today I think he is scheduled to learn about the lives of frogs." She reached out to take hold of Stewart's arm. "Come walk me to the door, dear."

Stewart didn't want to go. He looked back at his friends. "Watch me," he wanted to say. "Don't let her zap me." He said nothing. Somehow, he made his feet move and his hand reach out to open the door for her.

"Get to school early in the morning, Stewart," she said when she had stepped outside, and there was no asking tone to her voice. "Yes, get to school in time to come by my room. I need to talk to you, and, dear, come alone. Don't bring Andrew, Rachel, or the onions."

"Woe is me," said Stewart to Rachel and Ham when the woman was gone. "I am undone."

· FIVE ·

Wait for me in the library," Stewart told Ham when they were inside the building the next morning. "If I don't make it back, you can have my iPod." He was only half kidding. Very few kids were in the hall that early, and Stewart imagined the sound of his footsteps on the wooden floor echoed along with the sound of his heartbeat.

"Stewart!" Ms. Gibbs seemed almost surprised to see him. "How nice of you to come." She smiled at him.

He shrugged. "You told me to come. I thought . . . you know, that I had to."

"Well," she said, "come sit beside me while we talk." She walked to her desk and pointed to a bright red over-stuffed chair near the desk chair. The chair had not been there yesterday, and Stewart wondered if she had zapped it up just for him. He bent to run his hand across the seat before he sat down.

"I'll get right to the point. You know I offered to help you with Taylor and your basketball playing." She paused. Stewart held onto the edge of the red chair and nodded his head. "Let's start with basketball. You have a game after school today, don't you?" He nodded again. "The thing is, Stewart, that I feel you may just lack confidence. Don't you suppose that might be your problem?"

"Well, sure, I guess so." Stewart had a strange feeling, like he was dreaming the entire conversation.

Ms. Gibbs put one hand up to touch her green necklace. "I'll tell you something, Stewart, when you are playing just glance up at me. I think just seeing me might remind you to have confidence in yourself. I'll sit on the first row of bleachers, so you will have no trouble seeing me." She stood then, but Stewart didn't move.

"You may go now, Stewart. Go find Ham. I'm sure he is waiting for you, right?"

Stewart nodded, and she said, "Oh, you're welcome, Stewart. You did say thank you, didn't you?" Stewart nodded again.

Stewart stepped out into the hall, but he couldn't think where he intended to go. He heard laughter and saw two boys shoving each other. Getting out of their way crossed his mind, but he didn't move. A body pushed against him. His backpack slipped from his shoulder, and he fell against the wall. Bending to pick up his pack, he remembered that he was supposed to meet Ham in the library.

Rachel was there with Ham, sitting at a table near the door. "What happened?" Ham reached out to take the backpack Stewart was almost dragging.

"Sit down." Rachel pulled out a chair beside her for him.

He took the chair, then motioned to Ham. "Lean over here. I don't want to talk loud." Ham half crawled over the table, and Stewart drew in a breath. "She wants to help me." His words came out in a hoarse whisper.

"With what?" Rachel asked.

"Basketball and . . . stuff."

"Wow!" Ham relaxed back into his chair.

The bell rang. Rachel and Ham pushed away from the table, but Stewart didn't move. "Wait." He put a hand out toward each of them. "What am I going to do?"

"We'll talk at lunch," said Rachel, and she hurried away.

Ham waited for Stewart to get up, and they left the library together. Just before they separated for first period, Ham put his hand on Stewart's arm. "You didn't tell about Taylor," he said.

"Huh?" Stewart pulled away.

"You left out the part about helping you get Taylor to like you, didn't you?"

"Don't mention that in front of Rachel, Ham. Rachel wouldn't like it, and we need her help to figure this all out." Ham didn't say anything. "Okay? You hear me, Ham?"

Ham shrugged. "Okay, okay. Don't get excited."

"Sure," said Stewart. "Getting involved with a witch isn't anything to get worked up over." He turned to go toward English class.

Somehow, he kept his mind on the lesson about gerunds, and he was surprised by how interested he was in the earthquake discussion in science class. How could he concentrate on school right now? Maybe Ms. Gibbs had already cast a spell on him. "There she is," Ham said to Stewart as they walked toward third period art class.

Stewart didn't say anything, couldn't form a word in his totally dry throat. Ms. Gibbs stood beside the door and watched them move toward her. Squirming, he imagined her eyes shot fiery darts into his body. He ducked his head, studying his shoes as he shuffled forward. Even Ham was quiet. Just before they got to the room, Stewart dropped back to follow Ham.

He was so close to Ms. Gibbs that their shoulders almost touched, but he did not look up. "How nice to see you, Stewart, or is it Wart?" Her words were almost a whisper. She reached out, and for just a half second, she touched his shoulder, ever so lightly. "You must decide, you know."

It was the longest class Stewart had ever suffered through. Each time Ms. Gibbs turned his way, he pretended to be absorbed in drawing. He put his energy into hoping she did not come to stand beside him, and she did not.

When the bell rang, Stewart bolted out the door, leaving his art stuff for Ham to put away. He headed straight to the cafeteria. Ms. Gibbs wouldn't come in there to talk to him in front of everyone. Still, he kept looking back as he stood in line. He chose an empty table and sat facing the door. He did not want to be surprised. After what seemed like a long time, Rachel and then Ham came to join him.

"Did she say anything to you?" Stewart asked when Ham had dropped his tray on the table.

"Nope. Didn't even look my way." Ham sat down. "You going to eat that corn dog?"

"No, but don't get any ideas about the chocolate cake."

"What we have to get ideas about," said Rachel, "is a plan of action."

"I'm even half hoping I don't get to play in the game at all." Stewart started on the cake. "I don't want her putting some kind of spell on me." He shifted on the cafeteria bench. "Do I?"

Ham shrugged. "Look at it this way, if she's determined to help you, why not go along with it? I mean, it isn't like you have much choice about having her in your life. You might as well get some good from it."

"Or some proof," said Rachel. "If you go along with her, maybe we can get some proof that she's a witch." She twisted her face. "You know, I've got a feeling her power has something to do with that green necklace. She's never without it." She nodded decidedly. Stewart studied his plate and wished he could be as certain of anything as Rachel always was.

In gym class Coach Knox was all hyped up over the game. He even called the team, "men" in an effort to build their confidence. "When you're out on the court this afternoon in the middle of the action, remember you're a Ram, and you're representing us all," he said in a tone like they were going out to save the nation. "It's a big responsibility."

"Don't look so worried, Wart," said Brad to Stewart under his breath. "You probably won't have to be in the middle of the action. Not much happens on the bench."

Stewart just looked at him. He wondered why Brad had turned so mean, but maybe it was just so he could use the nickname. Stewart had to admit the use of that name would be hard to resist. Oh well, Brad couldn't get to him, not now. What did Brad Wilson know about action? Had he ever battled a witch?

The game was right after school. Stewart kind of got into the spirit of things during the warm-up, really felt pretty good out there in his red and blue uniform, representing the whole school. He enjoyed passing the ball and shooting even though he only made it once out of five times. Then he saw his father come in with Ms. Gibbs. Stewart hadn't mentioned the game to his father. Why should he? He certainly didn't expect to get to play. Ms. Gibbs must have told him. Dad waved at him, and

Ms. Gibbs gave him a thumbs-up sign. Stewart turned away and pretended he hadn't noticed. Out of the corner of his eye he saw them settle on the very first row, just where she had told him she would be. Stewart didn't feel so good anymore.

Brad was right about Stewart not seeing much action. For the first three quarters he warmed the bench. Even Ham got to play while Brad picked at the dirt under one fingernail with the nails on the other hand. About the middle of the last quarter when it was pretty certain the team was going to lose anyway, Coach motioned for Stewart. "Come on," he said, "you can go in for Brad."

Stewart's heart was pounding. Brad gave him a dirty look when he touched his hand to signal that Brad was being replaced, but Stewart didn't care. It was his first time to play in a real ball game, and he liked the feeling. Without even thinking about it, he glanced at Ms. Gibbs. She waved to him, then rubbed her green necklace.

That's when it started! The other team had just put up an unsuccessful shot. Time for the rebound. Suddenly, like he was jet-propelled, Stewart shot up above the others and grabbed the ball. It was as good as a dream, the way he drove down that court, moving from right to left, dodging their defense, like the other players were kindergartners. He made that layup so easily, him, Stewart Wright!

The crowd was cheering really loud, but the miracle wasn't done. The kid who took the ball out threw it way over Stewart's head. Somehow he jumped higher than he had ever imagined he could, intercepting the pass. That ball felt perfect in his hand, a natural part of him. He started toward the basket, but they were all around him, five of them, determined to block another layup.

A quick glance at the clock told him seconds were precious. There was no one to pass to. A shot from that far was ridiculous, but what else was there to do. For a split second, he glanced toward Ms. Gibbs. He aimed and threw. The ball swished into that net like it had been programmed by a computer.

"Yeah, Stewart! He's our man!" He'd know that cheerleader's voice anywhere. It was Taylor Montgomery.

"The buzzer sounded. Stewart's team had lost the game, but his three points made the score much more respectable.

Most of the guys gathered around him. Even Brad slapped him on the back. "Great lucky streak, Wart," he said.

"Coach should have put you in a lot sooner," said Jake.

As Stewart walked off the court, the coach motioned him to come over to the bench. Coach put one foot up on the bench, and he put an arm around Stewart's shoulder. "Good going, Wright," he said, "real good going."

Stewart's head was swimming as he headed for the dressing room. It really was like a dream, and he remembered the one he'd had the week before about him and Ham's grandmother winning the race. You couldn't have played like that by yourself, a voice whispered in his mind, but Stewart didn't want to think about Ms. Gibbs. He wanted to enjoy what had just happened.

The coach talked to them before they got dressed. "We lost the first one, men," he said, "but we learned some things about our strengths and weaknesses." Stewart could feel some of the guys looking at him.

After the talk, Stewart started to change his clothes. He had untied one basketball shoe when Ham dropped the bombshell. "Well, looks like Ms. Gibbs is a witch, all right. We've still got to get close enough to spy."

While Ham talked, Stewart didn't move, just stayed bent over halfway to the floor. He felt cold, like he'd just been thrown into an icy pool. Ms. Gibbs! He had to admit to himself that she was behind his great improvement on the court. Still, he didn't want to talk about it, not even to Ham.

"Right," was all he said. He fastened his attention on untying and tying his shoes like he was just learning. He did not want to think, but the glow inside him was definitely less bright. Coming up the steps from the dressing room, Stewart kept his gaze down. He didn't want to look toward where Dad and Ms. Gibbs were probably still sitting, waiting for him. When he was on the top step, his father's voice forced him to look up. "Here's our star," he said, and Stewart was surprised to see it was Martha, not Ms. Gibbs who waited with his father.

He wanted to run to Martha and hug her, but instead he gave her a big smile. "Wow," he said, "I didn't know you were here."

"I came in near the end, but I saw the important part." She reached out and gave him a quick hug. Stewart wanted to hold on to her and beg her to marry his dad and come home with them.

His father reached over to punch him on the shoulder. "Some game, Stew," he said. "Wanda had to leave, but she wanted me to congratulate you for her."

Stewart ignored the mention of Wanda Gibbs and smiled at his father. He felt good. Dad was pleased over his playing well because he knew it made Stewart feel good. He wasn't one of those fathers pushing his kid to be an athlete so he'd have something to brag about to his friends. Dad had always been great to him, no matter what. Stewart resolved to tell Ms. Gibbs he didn't want her help anymore. He didn't want her near his father either.

He decided to make a suggestion. "Hey," he said, "let's go home and get Georgia and all go out to eat. Gran can put tonight's supper in the fridge." He could see from the look on Martha's face that she liked the idea. They both looked at his father.

"Georgia's missed you." His father looked down, embarrassed.

"We all have," Stewart added quickly.

"Yes," Dad laughed, and he seemed to relax. "We've all missed you."

"Let's go to the Stagecoach," Dad suggested. "We'll meet you there after we pick up Georgia." It was a burger place where all the booths were shaped like stagecoaches.

"You know," said Martha to Stewart and Georgia at the restaurant when their father went to the restroom, "this is where your father and I came for our first meal together. It wasn't a date, just a chance to grab a bite after a meeting we were in together." Her voice sounded sad.

Stewart felt miserable. "Martha," he said, "I'm sorry I didn't want you to marry Dad. I was acting like a baby."

His hand rested on the table, and Martha reached out to pat it. "You've grown up a lot lately, haven't you?" she said.

Dad came back just in time to hear that. "He really is growing up, isn't he?" Georgia played quietly with her toy horse while the others spent some time then talking about Stewart's future. It wasn't just pressure talk about making good grades. Martha and Dad were asking questions about his interests and making suggestions about professions.

"You've always loved history," said his father. "You might want to be a college professor, too, or work in a museum."

Georgia looked up from her play. "You could be a doctor."

"Nah," Stewart shook his head. "I don't like blood."

"Well, then you could be a psychologist," suggested Martha.

"Would you treat me for free?" His father grinned slightly.

"I'm not sure you can wait that long, Dad," Stewart said.

They were all laughing when the waitress came to take their order. "It's nice to see a happy family," she said. They didn't correct her, just smiled at each other.

Stewart hated to see the meal come to an end. They all walked out together. It was a beautiful fall night. Stewart moved as slowly as he could, hoping that Dad would say something about seeing Martha again, but he didn't.

All the way to the car, Stewart kicked at a small rock in the parking lot. Before getting into the car, he gave it one last kick and watched it bounce under the car parked beside theirs. No one said much on the way home. He started thinking, of course, about Ms. Gibbs. Had she really made him play so well? When he was on the court, did she rub that necklace of hers? He wondered if she would be powerless if she lost that thing like Rachel seemed to think. Was there a chance they could get their hands on that green stone? "Necklace." He said it aloud without realizing it until his father spoke.

"What?"

He had to think quickly. "Reckless, I was just saying I can't get reckless with the ball because I made one three-pointer. Even though it was dark, he had to turn away from his father. Lying wasn't his best skill.

"Oh, I don't know." Dad laughed. "They'll probably be calling you Magic Wright pretty soon."

Stewart put his head back against the seat. "It did seem like magic, all right." Of course, his father had no idea what he meant. It wouldn't do him any good to try another round at convincing him that Ms. Gibbs was a broom rider. He had to get proof, had to get his hands on that necklace. But how?

"Think I'd better go up and hit the algebra book," Stewart said when they got home. At least that was the truth. He had an algebra test tomorrow. The idea of being a psychologist had been just talk, but something about it had sparked his interest. Anyway, it was true that he was going to high school next year, and it was time to get serious about his schoolwork.

The next day started off great. Stewart had just put his books in his locker when he realized Taylor was standing beside him. He was so shocked he could barely get out a "hi."

"I liked watching you play yesterday." She was wearing a blue sweater, and he thought she must be the most beautiful girl on the planet.

"Thanks."

"I'm having some kids over on Friday night, you know Halloween." She leaned on the locker next to his. "Are you doing anything?"

"I . . . I don't think so." He closed the locker door pretty hard on his hand, but it didn't even hurt.

"Don't injure yourself." She was batting her eyes at him. "The team needs you. I mean, really!" Then she was gone.

"Don't injure yourself," said a mocking voice from behind him. He turned to see Rachel glaring at him. "No, don't injure yourself. Let me do it for you!"

"Hey what are you so fired up about?"

"Stewart Wright," she had her face screwed up really tight. "If you think I'm going to be over at the Gibbs's place risking my life on Halloween night while you trot off to spend the evening making eyes at Taylor Montgomery, you're even crazier than I thought you were." Without waiting for him to say anything, she stomped off.

"Oh wow." He rested against his locker. His life had sure become complicated since the day Mr. Harrison went bonkers and climbed into the supply closet.

At lunch he tried to smooth it over with Rachel. He held out his hand to stop her when she started to walk by the table where he sat with Ham. "Wait," he said, "you didn't give me a chance to explain. Sit down, so we can talk."

Rachel settled across from him, but her face was not friendly. She sat there leaning on her elbows, one eyebrow raised. Her brown eyes made him feel uncomfortable, partly because she was glaring at him, but partly too because for the first time ever a strange thought came to his mind. Rachel was pretty! Really pretty. He wasn't quite comfortable with the thought.

He gave his head a slight shake to clear his mind. "I didn't know for sure that you guys were really planning to go to Ms. Gibbs's house on Friday night, but if you are, of course I'll go too."

"That's good of you." Rachel rolled her eyes.

"We haven't even talked about what to do over there," said Ham.

"I know what we'll do," said Stewart. His voice was strong, and there was a tone of determination to it. It was, he noticed, enough to make Rachel warm up. She leaned toward him. "The necklace," he said. "We're going for that necklace."

"That's her power. I'm sure of it." Rachel had totally forgotten about being mad.

Stewart pounded his fist against the table. "Okay, team," he said, "let's get that necklace!"

Before anyone had a chance to say anything, Stewart felt a touch on his shoulder. "Oh, Stewart," Taylor said, "I wanted to say you could bring your friends." She used her hand to indicate she meant Rachel and Ham. "Andrew, isn't it, and Ruby?"

"You can call me Ham. It's my nickname on account of my last name being Hamilton." Ham grinned up at Taylor.

"And you can call me Rachel." There was no smile on her face. "On account of it's my name, as you hear every day in English and geography class."

"Sorry," said Taylor, "but anyway, Stewart, you can bring your friends, whatever their names are. The more the merrier, right?" She patted Stewart's shoulder and without waiting for an answer she moved away. He had to pull his gaze from her swaying hips.

"Man oh man, we've been invited to Taylor Montgomery's party. Are we going?" Ham's voice sounded hopeful.

"We are not," said Rachel. "She knows my real name." She made a face like she tasted something bad. "No one can be that stupid." Then she shrugged her shoulders. "Or maybe you guys think we should drop everything and run over to Taylor's. After all, Stewart might like living with a witch and a frog."

Women! Stewart groaned inwardly. Sometimes he thought they were all witches, but he certainly didn't say anything. He really, really needed Rachel. Why did Rachel hate Taylor? Maybe he'd write to Sammi to see if she could explain it.

Stewart was on his way to algebra when he looked up to see Ms. Gibbs coming toward him. What the heck, he thought, why shouldn't he give it a try? It would be a way to find out for sure if she was a witch. He took a deep breath. "Ms. Gibbs." It was the first time he had ever started a conversation with her, and she seemed surprised and pleased, giving him a big smile.

"You should call me Wanda. Of course, not in class, but when we're alone."

"I was thinking about, you know, what you said." He was beginning to get itchy all over. Maybe it was nerves, but he wondered if she was causing it.

"What was that, Stewart? I'm not sure I know what you mean."

He wasn't sure he knew what he meant either. Of course she had on that necklace, all sparkling like her eyes. "About helping me and everything." His head itched so badly he had to scratch it.

So there he was standing in the hall acting like a dog with fleas. "Are you referring to my offer to give you some pointers on girls or basketball?" She seemed less eager now to be his buddy.

"Yeah, both, sort of." Stewart scratched around his waist. "Except that what I really need help with right now is algebra. We're having a test next period."

"Stewart," she sounded like just a regular teacher, not someone who wanted to be his mother. "I don't know a thing about math. It's been years since I had math. A liberal arts major, you know. Besides," she frowned and shook her head in disapproval, "don't you think it is a little late to ask for help with a test next period?"

Stewart scratched his neck and felt like a total idiot. "But the game. You helped me, didn't you?"

"Do you mean the basketball game?" She was looking at him strangely. "Are you talking about what I said about giving you confidence?" Stewart nodded. "Do you think that helped you? Oh, I'm so glad. That's all I could have done to help you. I wish I knew more about the game, but I have never played or paid much attention to it." She started to back away from him. "It was lovely to talk with you dear, but we both need to get to class now."

Great move, Wart, Stewart said to himself as he moved down the hall. What did all that mean? All he had done was confuse himself more and fill his head with things to interfere with thinking clearly for his test. At least the horrible itching stopped as suddenly as it had started. Actually, Stewart was a little disappointed about that. The idea of being sent home for having lice and missing the test had come to his mind.

Mr. Payne stood at the door of the algebra classroom. "Ready for your test?" He sounded almost gleeful, like a man who enjoys watching others suffer, and Stewart thought, as he had often before, that *pain* was a perfect name for an algebra teacher.

"I'm hoping for a little magic," Stewart muttered, and made his way to his seat. He received no magic. Every answer was a struggle, especially the second page of equations. God, Stewart was certain, never meant for man to mix numbers and letters. When he finished he took his paper up to the desk, and Mr. Payne graded it right then. "C minus," he announced. "An improvement, but not exactly magic. Work a little harder."

Yeah, Stewart thought, work a little harder. Work at algebra, work at getting Taylor to like me without making Rachel hate me, work at basketball, and most of all work at keeping a woman who might be a witch from marrying my dad. He could see the headline in the paper, BOY WORKS HIMSELF TO DEATH.

He was pretty down by gym class. Coach Knox gave him a private pep talk just before they started to scrimmage. "Wright, I'll have my eye on you. Give us your all, like you did in the game." Just then Stewart looked up to see Ms. Gibbs step into the gym. Because last period was her preparation period, she was free to watch practice, but it definitely was unusual.

Things started off great, with Stewart stealing the ball from Brad and passing to Jake who made a basket. Next, he stuffed the shot a player on the other team was about to make. When he got his hands on the ball, he drove in and made a great layup. Boy was he on a roll.

Then his luck changed. He missed a pass aimed right at him. Next he walked with the ball, like a kid who had never heard the rules. Once Ham passed him the ball when he was wide open for a perfect shot. He put up the ball with confidence, but it went over the backboard. He whirled around to look up in the stands. Ms. Gibbs was gone.

Later in the dressing room, Stewart waited for a chance to talk to Ham. "Did you notice, Ham? When she left, my luck sure took a nosedive." Ham nodded.

Coach Knox didn't say anything to Stewart on the way out. He turned his back and started to gather up the balls.

"I've got to know," Stewart told Ham on the way out of the gym. "I can't take this up and down business. If Ms. Gibbs is messing in my life, I have to prove she's a witch. We're going to her house Friday night, and we're getting our hands on her necklace."

"How? She always wears it."

Stewart stopped walking. "We'll get it even if we have to hide in her closet until she goes to sleep. Surely she doesn't sleep in the thing." He began to move again.

"You talking about spending the night in Ms. Gibbs's house?" Ham's eyes were big with surprise.

"Well," Stewart hesitated. "I guess I am." Then with a determined nod of the head, he said, "It's the only way. You're with me, aren't you?"

At first Ham didn't answer. His head was turned away, and Stewart wondered if maybe he hadn't heard. "Ham," Stewart gave his shoulder a little shove. "Ham, you're with me, right?"

"Well, sure. The thing is I was just thinking about Rachel. She's a girl, you know."

Stewart looked at his friend. "Yeah, Ham, I've known about Rachel being a girl since we were babies. You know, the pink and blue thing? What's your point here?"

"Well, she might be afraid," Ham said. He did not look at Stewart.

Stewart was pretty sure Ham wanted Rachel to refuse to go, hoping Stewart would then drop the idea. He didn't say anything to Ham. No one wanted to be called a coward. Besides, it didn't seem likely that Rachel would be afraid. The truth, though, was that he had never really thought of Rachel as a girl, not until she got so angry about Taylor Montgomery. Could it be that Rachel thought of him as a potential boyfriend? That would be weird.

While they walked home, Stewart thought about Taylor and how she had finally noticed he was alive. Was that because of some spell? How would he feel if it was? Even without closing his eyes he could imagine Taylor leaning against his locker inviting him to her house for a party. But he couldn't go. Maybe somehow he'd get another chance with Taylor.

"Taylor's party is out," he told Ham just before they separated in front of Stewart's house. "We've got to put all our energy into the witch hunt."

"Oh well," Ham said, "You would probably just have gotten beat up anyway. Brad has the hots for Taylor real bad. Anyone can see that. He might just kill you if Taylor shows any interest in you."

Stewart moved up the walk to his house. So, Brad was likely to kill him. "Thanks for sharing that bit of bright news," he called to Ham, then walked into the house.

< 100 >

·SIX·

The rest of the week went by pretty fast because they had a lot of planning to do. When Stewart told Taylor he couldn't come to her party, she seemed to be truly disappointed. He had stopped her in the hall. "Oh," she said. "That's too bad." She reached out and sort of pinched his cheek. "We'll just have to find some other way to get better acquainted, won't we?"

"Sure," he said. Then she went on into her English class. It was all Stewart could do to keep from following her like he had that first time he had really noticed her.

After that Stewart did everything he could to keep his mind off Taylor and on what lay ahead. The first problem was to work out things with his father. "You got any plans for Friday night?" he asked on Wednesday evening while they were folding laundry.

"Well, Wanda and I were thinking of making it a

family evening. Maybe take Georgia and Ozgood trick or treating, come back here and watch movies, make some candy apples or something."

It didn't sound like much of a Halloween for a witch and her little warlock. Maybe Ham was right about real witches not paying special attention to that day, or maybe the action didn't start until after midnight. Stewart put his stack of towels in the basket. "I was sort of planning to spend the night at Ham's," he said. Lying was getting to be a habit.

"Why not have him here?" Dad stood up to fold a sheet. "If we do the family thing, I want you to be around."

"I want to spend the night with Wendy," Georgia protested. "We're going to play witches and black cats. We're going to play like we turn Wendy's little brother into a toad because he's too little to know anything. They've got a black cat." She took a deep breath. "Me and Wendy are going to play lost children, too, and we're going to trick-or-treat at all the houses on her block." She went over to pull at Dad's leg. "Please, Wendy's mother is going to call you tonight."

Dad gave a little shrug. "If she calls, you can go, I suppose. Wanda will understand. Of course, Ozgood may be a little disappointed."

A brilliant idea came to Stewart. "I think Ham and I might go over to see Ozgood. Take the basketball and see if he wants to practice some handling techniques."

Dad was pleased. "That's very generous of you, son. Wanda will be glad."

Yeah, glad, Stewart thought. That is unless she finds out I'm about to ask her son to help me prove she's a witch.

"Daddy," said Georgia with a wistful voice. "Don't you think it would be fun if there really and truly was a witch, and she really truly did ride a broom and really truly did have black cats for helpers and everything?"

"And could really truly turn strange little boys into frogs," Stewart added, but his father's threatening look kept him from going on.

"I thought you were coming around to being reasonable," he said in a voice that told Stewart he had better be.

"I am," he said. "It was just a momentary slip, just a joke." Stewart gave his father a big grin, but Dad didn't grin back, just handed him a stack of laundry to put away.

The next day before art class started, Stewart asked Ms. Gibbs about coming over to see Ozgood.

"I'd like to get to know him better," he said, but he did not look directly at the woman as he spoke.

"Me too." Ham was standing just behind Stewart. "Me and Stewart don't have any brothers, just sisters. He's real excited about maybe having a little brother."

She giggled like a young girl. "Why, Stewart, has your father said anything to give you such an idea? We've never discussed marriage. It seems too early."

"Oh," Stewart ducked his head. "I guess I shouldn't

have said anything. Dad likes you a lot." He shrugged. "That's all, and me and Georgia, well, we're starting to get our hopes up, I guess."

"You dear, dear boy," she said, and Stewart was afraid she might hug him. "By all means come over after school. I'll make cookies. Do you need a ride?"

Stewart and Ham looked at each other. For a second, a picture flashed through Stewart's mind, Ham and he riding behind Ms. Gibbs on a broom. "We'll ride our bikes," he said, and Ham nodded his head.

Ozgood was waiting outside for the boys. "All right," he said, "for what purpose did you come?" He pushed up his glasses, put his head back slightly, and studied Stewart's face. He folded his arms across his chest.

"We came to see you, old buddy." Stewart moved to stand beside him then put his arm around Ozgood's shoulders. "Thought we might pass the basketball some." He pointed to the ball in the basket of his bicycle.

"I don't care for basketball or for pretense." Ozgood turned his head away, but Stewart thought he saw the beginning of tears in his eyes, and his conscience hurt.

"Okay," he said. "It wasn't very nice of us to pretend we just wanted to be your friends. We're going to tell you the truth, aren't we, Ham?"

Ham rolled his eyes and shrugged his shoulders. "Hey," he said, "this is your deal and your stepbrother to be." He walked back to the bike to get the ball.

"Okay," Stewart said again, trying to think how to go on. He had to be careful. "It's true that we came to ask you for a favor, but it's also true that we like you." Suddenly, he realized the truth of his words. Ozgood was just a little boy, who seemed very lonely. "We want to be your friends."

"I've never had a friend," he said, and Stewart thought he didn't look like a warlock at all, just a sad kid.

"You've got two now," said Ham.

"What is the favor you seek?" Ozgood walked to the big porch swing to sit down. Ham and Stewart settled on either side of him.

"Ozgood," Stewart put his arm around him again and pressed his shoulder. "Tell us the truth now, please. Is your mother really a witch?" When Ozgood didn't answer right away, Stewart gave him another squeeze. "Tell us," he pleaded.

"Do you believe in such things?" Ozgood turned his face up to Stewart and from behind his glasses his eyes gave Stewart a long, searching look.

"I don't know," said Stewart, and for once he was aware of telling the absolute truth.

"I believe," said Ham. "At least I do if you say your mother is one, because I don't think you would tell us something that wasn't the truth."

"Well, then, believe this," Ozgood said. "I will be severely punished if I discuss this with you." He folded his arms across his chest again, and Stewart could tell the subject was closed.

"Let's play some ball," Stewart said. In a few minutes he realized he had forgotten that Ozgood didn't like basketball, but it seemed to him that Ozgood must have forgotten too because he smiled while the boys passed the ball with him. While they showed him how to dribble on the driveway, his smile grew even bigger.

After a while, Ms. Gibbs came to the door and called them in for cookies and milk. The cookies were homemade and delicious. As he ate them, Stewart started to wonder if the whole thing could be a crazy joke Ozgood had started. Would a witch serve cookies and milk and be so happy because her little boy had someone to show him how to pass a ball?

"Ask him about Friday night," Ham whispered to Stewart when Ms. Gibbs left the room, but Stewart waited until they were ready to go.

Ozgood walked out with them. "Ozgood," Stewart said, "I've got to know the truth about your mother. If you won't talk to us about it, will you give us a chance to find out for ourselves?"

Ozgood pushed up his glasses. "Using what method?"

"Let us in your house Halloween night. We want to hide in your mother's closet until after she goes to bed," said Ham.

Ozgood looked shocked. "You wish to watch my mother disrobe?"

"No, no," Stewart said, "we wouldn't do that! We just want to look at her necklace, you know the green one she always wears. We want to examine it."

"We won't hurt it," said Ham.

"The necklace? You want to look at it? Do you plan to take it home with you?"

"If we do, we will bring it back," said Stewart.

"I don't think taking the necklace would be wise. I don't think I should have anything to do with your plan." Ozgood stepped back toward the door.

Stewart put his hand on Ozgood's arm. "You don't want your mother to marry my father, do you?"

Ozgood smiled slightly. "You would be my brother then, though, wouldn't you?"

Stewart could see that Ozgood was starting to like the idea. "But we might have more fun as friends," he said, and he looked at Ham to mouth, "Help!" when Ozgood glanced away.

"There's Georgia to consider," Ham said. "She's not easy to live with." He shook his head. "I can tell you, I'd hate to try to live in the same house as that girl."

"That's right," Stewart put in quickly, "and she's scared to death of things. You'd have to give up all your monster stuff and bones and everything. That kid is so easy to scare. We've got this new neighbor, nice old lady, but her name is Mrs. Wolf. My little sister won't go near her house, insists on calling her, 'the wolf,' like in big, bad wolf." That part was true, but then Stewart began to make things up. "Dad gets real worried about her, makes sure she is never exposed to anything scary at all."

"Your music would have to go," said Ham. He turned

to Stewart, "I wonder if your dad would even let Ozgood wear those neat pajamas anymore."

"Oh no," Stewart shook his head sadly, "the pajamas would definitely have to go."

Ozgood let out a deep sigh. "What time shall I expect you to arrive?"

Stewart's heart raced. They were going to get into the house. "What time do you think we should come?"

"I'm to have a babysitter while your father takes Mother out to dine."

"Hey," said Ham, "why couldn't we hide in Ozgood's room, wait until his mom is sleeping, and then sneak into her room?"

"You could stay outside, near my window, and await my signal." Ozgood's voice was full of excitement, and the boys knew he was getting into the sprit of the adventure. "When an opportune moment arises, I could let you in the back door."

"We'll be there about nine," Stewart said.

"Three quick blinks of my light," Ozgood said, and he put out his hand for shaking to Stewart and then to Ham.

From Ozgood's they went straight to see Rachel. "We will all wear black," she said. "That way no one will see us waiting outside." No one else was home, and Rachel walked the family room floor as she spoke.

"Food," said Ham. "We'll need lots of it, not just chips, something serious like sandwiches. Got to keep our strength up."

Rachel grabbed a pad and pencil from beside the telephone. "A flashlight, of course, and a camera in case we need a picture of evidence, perhaps a small tape recorder."

Rachel studied her list, thinking about what else they would need. Ham planned the menu. Stewart swallowed hard. His friends were busy, so was he—busy trying not to think, trying not to face what they were about to get into. He looked at the pillows covering one end of the couch and wanted to hide his head under them.

At school on Friday, Stewart moved in a sort of trance. It's lucky, he thought during lunch, that nothing important was happening today. At least, he didn't think it was. After school he explained to his father that Ham and he were going to hang out at their house first and end up at Ham's. He knew Ham was telling his folks that they would be at Stewart's. Rachel planned to tell her folks she was going to a slumber party at her friend Ashley's house.

Stewart worried about phone calls. Rachel would have her cell phone. If her parents wanted her, they would call it. Like Stewart, Ham didn't have a cell phone. If Stewart or Ham should get a phone call from home, the plan would be ruined.

As soon as Mr. Wright pulled out of the drive, Rachel and Ham showed up.

"Let's watch TV to get our minds off what's about to happen," Stewart said, but after flipping through the channels, he gave up the hope of finding anything they could really get into.

Ham passed quite a bit of time raiding the refrigerator, making sandwiches and filling a small ice chest with cans of soda. "Hey, Stew, will your dad say anything about the missing food?" he called from the kitchen.

"Nah, he's used to that when you're over here. We've got a lot more to worry about than an empty fridge." A new worry came up around eight. They were about to begin the thirty-minute walk across town when they heard a loud roll of thunder.

Stewart stepped out of the sunroom room door onto the deck and stepped right back in very wet. "It's pouring," he said.

"We may have to give this up," said Ham, and Stewart could see the hope in his eyes.

"No," said Rachel. "Get us some raincoats."

"All I have is one all-weather jacket." Stewart wiped water from his arms with a paper towel. "We don't usually go for long walks during rainstorms."

"Trash bags," said Rachel. "Two for each of us."

They each wore one over their head with a face hole cut out. The others were tied around their waists like skirts. Rachel carried another bag filled with her equipment. Over his shoulder, Ham slung a trash bag with food in the bottom.

At first the walk was pretty miserable, rain hitting them in their faces and splashing up their jeans' legs.

About halfway through the journey, the drops got smaller and farther apart. The rest of the way was not so bad, just sprinkles.

"Bell Street," Rachel said when they came to a corner. "We're almost there." She leaned for a minute against the pole that held the street sign.

The house stood on the next corner. The front part of the first floor was bright, the second story dark. They were in the driveway before Stewart noticed the car. He stopped walking and reached out to grab the edge of the bags each of the others wore. "Wait," he said, "that's Martha's car!"

"Are you sure?" Rachel asked.

"Yes, that's hers all right." He pointed. "See the book bumper sticker. 'Take a book to bed.'"

They huddled together under a tree near Ozgood's window. Stewart couldn't stop thinking of Martha inside with Ozgood. "This doesn't make sense," he said. "Martha is in there babysitting while that woman goes out with the man she loves." He felt too tired to stand up. Leaning against the tree, he lowered himself to the wet grass.

Rachel and Ham sat down, too, and for a minute they were all quiet. Then Rachel said, "What're you thinking, Stew?"

"Martha wouldn't hang around with witches. I mean, she's a librarian. Nobody is as sensible as a librarian."

Ham started getting up. "Well," he said, "if you're thinking Ms. Gibbs isn't a witch, let's just go on home."

Rachel grabbed his garbage-bag skirt. "No," she said, "we came to get the necklace, and we're going to do it."

Just then the light went on in Ozgood's room. They could see two forms through the shade, and then the light went off again. "She tucked him in," said Rachel. "It won't be long now."

They waited without saying anything, barely breathing until the light came back on and went off three times. "It's time," said Rachel. They stood up and moved quietly toward the back door.

"Quickly," said Ozgood's voice in the dark. "Quickly and cautiously up to my room. The closet door is open."

Tiptoeing, they went through the kitchen into the dining room, where the stairs were. An open door separated the dining room from the family room, where Martha sat watching TV.

Their feet didn't make a sound as they crossed the room, but the rustling of their garbage bags seemed loud to Stewart. He held his breath. If Martha decided to get up or to turn down the sound, they were dead. Once they were up the stairs, he relaxed some. The first hurdle was over.

"We need to look over Ms. Gibbs's room," said Rachel, "see how things are arranged in there. The door was half open, and she pushed it wider. For a minute they all looked inside, then moved on.

Ham landed in the closet first, and the other two piled in after him. "We'll close the door at first," whispered

Rachel, "so we can use the flashlight, but after a bit, we'll have to open it for air."

The thought came to Stewart that Rachel had definitely become the leader, but he didn't mind a bit. He knew he was too nervous to think clearly. Ham took food from his bag and arranged it on the closet floor. They all ate. The sandwiches were sort of squashed, but they tasted good. Ozgood had politely pushed his bones into a corner, but Rachel, also a serious science student, pulled them out and started to examine them. While she ate, the bones rested beside her, a skull in her lap. Stewart thought it was a strange picture, but his life had changed so much that odd almost seemed normal.

After a while they switched off the light and opened the door just slightly. It wasn't long until they heard voices downstairs. None of them dared even whisper because the sounds were coming closer, up the stairs. Ham grabbed Stewart's arm. Feeling Ham shake made Stewart even more nervous, so he reached for Rachel's hand and held it. They sat there, crunched together in a terrified little pile.

A light from the hall told them that Ozgood's door was being opened. It was too late to close the closet. "I won't turn on the light," whispered Ms. Gibbs. "Just want to look in on him."

"He's a darling," said Martha. "And you are, too, Wanda. I'll never forget what you're doing for me, uprooting your life and Ozgood's to move here."

"Oh, don't thank me," said Ms. Gibbs, and she laughed. "I'm having fun. The man's a challenge. I'm just glad you called me for help."

Then the door closed and the two women went back down the stairs. In the closet, they quit holding onto each other, took deep breaths, and slipped off their garbage bags.

Stewart bent his head to rest on his raised knees. What was Martha talking about? What was Ms. Gibbs doing for her? Then a thought came to him. "Martha must be under a spell," he whispered. "That's the only thing that makes sense. Martha's under a spell and so is my dad."

"Maybe," said Rachel. "Do you think Ozgood is really asleep?"

"Surely, he didn't go to sleep, knowing we're hiding in here," said Ham, but Stewart pointed out that little kids sometimes went to sleep no matter what. After a long time, they heard Ms. Gibbs come upstairs and open her bedroom door.

"How long do you think it will take for her to get to sleep?" Stewart whispered.

"Not long, I hope," said Ham. "I've got to go to the bathroom."

"Put your plastic bag back on and wet your pants," said Rachel. "We aren't leaving this place for at least two hours." Ham groaned.

They settled back to wait. Rachel passed the time

touching the bones. Stewart decided to try to get his mind on a good Taylor Montgomery daydream. He settled on being the president of the United States, the youngest ever elected. Having lost track of Taylor, he had never married despite the fact that women swooned when he spoke.

Things were going along well until a bunch of people on a subway are taken hostage by some terrorists. No one in the country knows what to do, so of course they turn to President Wright. He looks at the passenger list and sees Taylor's name.

People beg him not to, but he is determined to trade himself for the hostages. Just before he is ready to leave, a note comes from Taylor. She says that the terrorists let her write it because she is about to die. She tells Stewart that she has always loved him, but that she had to drop out of his life because she thought she wasn't good enough for him.

He takes out his handkerchief and wipes his tears. There are a lot of reporters who want to take the president's picture while he cries over the hostages. "There is no time for tears or pictures," Stewart says. "This is the time for action!"

His advisers send for all kinds of bulletproof vests and stuff, but Stewart refuses them. "Bring me two garbage bags," he says. "They were the protection I wore on my first dangerous mission."

He was just at the good part where he burst onto the

train and Taylor held out her arms to him when Ham started to move. "I'm going to the john," he said.

"No," Rachel protested. "She may not be asleep."

"I'm going anyway." He pushed the closet door open wider.

"If he makes it to the bathroom, we might as well check out Ms. Gibbs's room. Maybe we can tell if she's asleep," Stewart suggested.

"Well, I don't know," Rachel said. "If we are going to do it, we have to plan first."

"Plan quick," Ham said.

"Okay, here's the deal." Rachel took the bones out of her lap and arranged them gently in the corner. "Ham, you go first. Don't turn on the bathroom light or flush the toilet. Stew and I will wait here just inside the room until we see you come back from the bathroom. If it is real quiet in there, we'll open the door just enough to crawl in." She breathed deeply. "Now let's see, there was a dresser, a bureau, and a nightstand. I'll check out the dresser top. There may be a jewelry box there. Ham, you take the bureau top, and Stew will do the nightstand. If one of us finds it, we just head out. The other two will follow."

"All right," said Stewart, "but what if we don't find it? What if it's in a drawer or still on her neck? What then?"

"Well," Rachel said, thinking. "Well, then we go into the closet and look for other evidence. I'll bring the camera and the flashlight."

Ham went first on his hands and knees. "You can

walk," whispered Rachel, but Ham stayed down. Stewart thought it was probably easier for Ham to control his strained bladder that way.

When Ham was out the bedroom door, Rachel and Stewart left the closet and moved to the doorway. As soon as Ham's dark form came out of the bathroom, they tiptoed toward Ms. Gibbs's room. Once there, they all dropped to their knees. The low sound of a train whistling through the crossing a few blocks away sent shivers down Stewart's spine, and when it passed, the sound of their breathing seemed to echo loudly against the walls of the hallway.

The door wasn't completely closed. Rachel gave it a little pull. They waited. Then an encouraging sound came from the room, regular little snorts. Ms. Gibbs was snoring. Even in the dark, Stewart could see Rachel make a thumbs-up sign. Then Ham and Stewart started stacking their hands on top of each other's, like for luck before a basketball game. Rachel caught on and joined them.

Rachel, of course, went first, then Stewart, followed by Ham. Stewart wished he still wore his garbage bags as a sort of armor but they'd make too much noise. They moved around the end of the bed. So far so good. Stewart was beside the nightstand. He put up his hand and began to slide it across the top of the little table. At first, he was afraid to look at Ms. Gibbs, asleep there in her bed. Then he took a quick glance. It wasn't too dark for him to see that she slept in some sort of netlike cap, which he supposed was to protect her hairdo. There was a bunch of white stuff smeared all over her face. Witch or not, he thought she was plenty scary looking at night.

Then he forgot all about how she looked because his fingers touched a chain. Slowly he pulled it to him. There was moonlight from the window, and it picked up the green shine. He held it up for a second, hoping the others would see. Then, still on his hands and knees, he started for the door. Holding the necklace in one sweaty fist, it was hard to crawl, so he jammed it into his pocket.

Suddenly, there was an extra big snort from Ms. Gibbs, and she flopped over in bed. "Hold still," she muttered. "Don't hop." Then she tossed herself over in bed again. Stewart froze. She was about to wake up. What should they do?

Rachel moved quickly, reaching for the closet door and getting it open. Ham moved quickly too. Ms. Gibbs turned noisily again in her bed, and Stewart knew she was likely to wake herself by talking in her sleep. Still, he couldn't move. When something touched his foot, he started with fright and almost yelled out. It was Rachel. She gave his foot a hard jerk, then shot back into the closet. Stewart followed, pulling the door after him.

"What was that?" called Ms. Gibbs, and Stewart thought her voice sounded awake. It was totally dark in the closet, but it didn't matter because Stewart kept his eyes shut tightly anyway. If Ms. Gibbs opened the closet door, he wanted no possibility of seeing her face. He lay there, aware that either Rachel or Ham was under him, aware of the chemical smell coming from the bottles on the shelf, but unable to move.

From the crack under the door came a ray of light, and they knew that Ms. Gibbs had switched on her lamp. Any second now she would get out of bed, cross to the closet, and find them. Then Stewart remembered what was in his pocket. Could she turn them into frogs without that necklace? A small thumping sound and a sort of metallic rattling could be heard. Then the light went off again. Was she going back to sleep? For a long time they didn't dare move. Then it started again, that marvelous, delightful sound of Ms. Gibbs snoring. In the closet the three moved about a little, getting off each other, but it was a long time before they dared to push open the door and start the long crawl to safety.

Outside the bedroom, they stood up and began to move more quickly, across the upstairs hall, down the stairs, through the dining room, into the kitchen. Ham reached for a cookie from a plate of them on the cabinet, but Stewart slapped his hand. It would have taken too long to get the plastic wrap from around the plate.

When the fresh night air hit their faces, they all broke into a run, not slowing until they were out of the Gibbses' yard. It was Rachel who stopped first, sort of throwing herself down on the curb. Stewart sat down beside her and was shocked to see that she was crying. "Rachel," he said, "what's the matter. Are you hurt?"

"Scared," she sobbed. "I was so scared."

He could feel her shaking beside him, and he put his arm around her. "Don't cry," he said. "We made it because you were so brave." Stewart felt a big smile come to his face. He felt good, like he was saving Taylor Montgomery from terrorists or something. "Let's look at the necklace," he said. He took his arm from around Rachel and began to dig into his pockets, first the right, then the left. He jumped up yelling, "Where is it? Help! Oh no! It's gone!" He whirled and reached down to grabbed Ham's shoulder. "I've lost the necklace."

Ham slumped, resting his head on his knees. "I know it," he said, "and I left our snacks in Ozgood's closet."

"Ham," Stewart yelled. "Forget the food. The necklace is gone!"

"It's okay," said Rachel, back to her competent self now. "It must have fallen from your pocket. We'll find it."

Rachel started crawling then, and the other two joined her, crawling through the wet grass in the Gibbses' yard, searching in the dark for a green stone. At the back porch they stopped. "Well," Rachel said, "it must be inside."

"Do we go after it?" Stewart asked.

"Sure." Ham already had his hand on the door. "We can't give up after all we've been through tonight."

"That's right," Rachel agreed, so they went inside. Retracing their path, they traveled on all fours across the kitchen, into the dining room, and up the stairs.

"I'll just go into Ozgood's room and get the food," Ham whispered. "Meet you guys outside."

Rachel and Stewart moved on to Ms. Gibbs's room. The sound of snoring came to their ears, and they knew the woman was sleeping. Slowly, Stewart pushed open the door. She was lying on her side, and this time Stewart looked at her right away.

Rachel looked right off too. Stewart knew that because she grabbed at him just as he was reaching for her, both of them pointing toward the sleeping woman. The moonlight was shining in brightly now. They could see her plainly, the net thing around her hair, the white goop on her face, and on her neck a chain with a shiny green stone.

Without pausing to close the door, they backed up just a little, stood, and made a tiptoeing dash for the stairs. Every little bit, Stewart turned back to make sure they weren't being followed.

· SEVEN ·

It was a miserable walk home. No one said anything except to complain about aching feet. Ham didn't even eat anything from the snack bag.

When they were finally there and inside the garage, Stewart looked at his watch to see that it was three o'clock. They climbed into the van, where they planned to sleep.

"You take the fold-out seat," Stewart said to Rachel. "We'll sleep on the floor."

Rachel took out the alarm clock from her equipment bag, set it, and said, "Good night."

"I'm giving up," Stewart said, and he closed his eyes. "There is no use trying to fight her."

"Might as well," said Ham. "Maybe she really will help you with stuff. Maybe she'll even help me if you ask her to."

"Stop it you two, and, Stewart Wright, don't you even think of giving up." Rachel sat up and shook her finger at Stewart. "You can't let a witch take over your family. We aren't beaten yet."

"Maybe she isn't a witch at all. Maybe she found the necklace," he said sadly. "Maybe she found it when she turned on the light. Remember the rattling noise we heard?"

"It found her," said Rachel, "and you know it." She lay back down.

Stewart didn't answer. There was nothing more, it seemed to him, to say. The next thing he knew the alarm was going off. He looked at the time, seven thirty. Dad was probably up and could be coming out to the garage any time. They climbed out, ready to go their separate ways. "Thanks," said Stewart. "Thanks, both of you. You were great."

"Anytime," said Rachel with a little laugh.

"Yeah," said Ham, "anytime in the next century!"

Stewart sat for a while on the front step, feeling dejected and alone. When he heard his father stirring in the house, he got out his key and went in with a story ready about waking up early at Ham's house and deciding to come on home.

His father was in a great mood, singing and joking. "Got any plans for the day?" He poured himself a cup of coffee.

"I'm pretty exhausted, not much sleep last night at

Ham's. I don't even want any breakfast. I just want to go to bed." It was true that he was sleepy, but he also figured his father was going to suggest some activity involving Ms. Gibbs. That was a face Stewart just couldn't look at again so soon. He headed out of the kitchen.

"Okay." Dad was taking eggs from the refrigerator. "Think I'll pick up Georgia, and if she's not too tired, we might go do a little Christmas shopping. We'll have our algebra lesson when I get home."

Stewart stopped and turned back to his father. "Christmas shopping? Last night was just Halloween."

"Well, sure it's early. Probably I won't buy anything, just look." He smiled at Stewart. "I think this will be our best Christmas ever."

He'll probably be married by December, Stewart thought with an inward groan. Then suddenly he remembered last Christmas, Martha helping them decorate the tree. Martha, he had to see her today. Maybe he would just level with Martha, ask her what Ms. Gibbs was doing for her. No, he couldn't admit hearing that. Still, he would go to talk to Martha. He would find a way to get information.

"Dad," he said, "after I wake up, I'd like to go over to the library to get a book and maybe talk to Martha a little."

"Sure, there's no reason Martha can't still be a friend of the family." Stewart thought his father's voice sounded a little sad.

"Dad," he said. "It was really stupid of me . . ." He paused and shrugged his shoulders slightly. "I mean not wanting you to marry Martha. I don't . . . maybe even after all that time I really hadn't, you know, accepted Mom's death."

His father was quiet for a second, just stood there with the eggs in his hand. Then he said, "It's okay, son. I guess I used you for an excuse. If I had really been ready for marriage, I wouldn't have waited for your approval." Dad smiled at him, and Stewart could see that his father thought their problems were over.

Stewart set his alarm for one. Then he fell into bed and went right to sleep. His dad and Georgia weren't home when he woke. After a nice long shower, he cooked a frozen pizza, scarfed it down, and was ready to go.

He got his bike from the garage, deciding to push it for a time before getting on, giving his muscles a chance to warm up. It was a good day for a bike ride. His father's remarks about Christmas shopping made him realize that he wouldn't have many more days like this one before winter. Well, he told himself as a red leaf drifted down to land on his face, today is an important day. The damp leaf had stuck to his face, and he did not remove it. Today he would decide what to do with his life. He could keep fighting like Rachel said he should, or he could just give in and quit being a worrywart. He felt very tired. If Dad wants to marry Ms. Gibbs, well, that's his business. Maybe he just wouldn't think about supernatural stuff. "Hey," he said aloud, "the woman makes great cookies."

"Cookies?" said a voice, and he saw Mrs. Wolf, their new neighbor, straighten up from behind her hedge. "Don't be pestering me for cookies. I gave them all away last night."

"Oh no, ma'am," he said. "I won't pester you." He got on his bike then and began to ride. "Maybe I won't pester anyone," he told the wind. He reached up to take the leaf from his face. "Maybe I'll turn over a new leaf."

He liked the way the library looked, made from some kind of white rock, and he liked the smell of it when he stepped inside. Martha was behind the desk, and Stewart saw her as soon as he came into the library. She was glad to see him, like always. "Stewart, good to see you. Did you come for a book on psychology?"

He opened his mouth to say yes because he was getting so used to lying, but he stopped himself. "No," he leaned on the big counter and looked at her warm, honest face. "I think maybe I'll get a book like that, but I came today to see you."

Tears came to her eyes, but she gave a little laugh. "Come on, now," she protested, "you've never been exactly wild about me." She shook her head. "Of course, there's no danger now of my stealing your father's attention."

"No, honest." Stewart leaned against the counter and he felt like crying too. He forced down the feeling. "I was wrong to act like a spoiled brat." He ducked his head for a second, then looked up again. "You would have been great."

"Oh, Stew," she said, wiping at her eyes, "that's good to hear even if it is too late."

Stewart wanted to ask her about Ms. Gibbs. He wanted to know what Martha would say if he just asked straight out about the witch thing, but the words wouldn't come. "Guess, I'll go now," he said, but she reached out to touch his arm.

"Wait, Stew," she looked right into his eyes. "Your father would have married me if he really wanted to. Don't blame yourself, but do give Wanda Gibbs a chance."

"I don't like that woman." He blurted out the words.

"Oh, Wanda is a little different, but she has a good heart. I should know! She's helped me plenty. If you had come in an hour earlier, you would have run into her. She was in here getting a book, and she talked to me about how much she thinks of you and Georgia." She smiled at him. "Believe me, Stew, things are going to work out for us all."

"She got a book?" he stalled, trying to think of how to ask his question.

"Yes, Wanda has developed an interest in poltergeists."

Stewart imagined his ears might be stretched up over his head. This was really interesting. "Does she believe in them?" He hoped his voice sounded casual.

Martha stacked a few books that were lying on the counter. "She doesn't know, but she told me an interesting story about something that happened to her last night."

"Really?" He put his hands in his pockets because he could feel them shaking and didn't want Martha to see. "What happened?"

Martha smiled. "I guess Wanda wouldn't mind my telling you. It seems she had a strange experience with a necklace. I babysat with Ozgood . . ." She paused.

"Go on," Stewart urged, then he realized he was showing too much interest. "I mean if you have time. I'm sort of interested in poltergeists."

"Well, after she came home, Wanda had taken off her green necklace. You may have noticed it, the one she wears a lot."

Stewart nodded and resisted the desire to urge her on.

"She says she is certain she put it on her nightstand. Then something woke her in the night. She decided to go to the bathroom, and several feet from her bed she felt an object under her foot. It was her necklace. She wonders how it could have moved and if the sound of that movement was what woke her." Martha gave a little laugh. "Who knows, maybe there really are such things as poltergeists? Anyway, Wanda has the book if you want to look at it. The fellow who wrote it believes in little spirits."

"Really?" It was all he could think to say.

"Yes," she stacked the last book, "and I think Wanda might too. She says she's going to sleep in the necklace from now on. It's very special to her because it belonged to her grandmother."

Stewart forgot all about the psychology book and wandered off after telling Martha good-bye. Right outside the library was a low brick wall, and he sat down on it. It was a place where kids liked to sit and wait for their rides. Usually they read the books they had just checked out. Stewart had no book, but he had to be still and think.

He sat for a long time. Several kids came to wait on the wall and were picked up, but Stewart hardly noticed them. Finally, he jumped down from the wall and got his bike. His mind was made up. Ms. Gibbs wouldn't have had to tell Martha a thing about the necklace. That meant, he was sure, that her story about finding it must be true.

He was anxious to talk to Rachel about what he had decided. She was in the front yard working with Molly Dot. The puppies were in a box on the front porch, their front paws and heads sticking up over the edge so they could watch their mother. Rachel took a dog treat from her pocket. She held it high with one hand. Then with the other hand also held high, she snapped her fingers. Molly sat up on her back legs. Rachel began to sing, "Patty cake, patty cake baker's man. Bake me a cake as fast as you can." All the time Rachel sang, Molly brought her paws together, over and over. When she quit singing, Molly dropped to all fours and Rachel gave her the treat.

"Wow!" Stewart said. "She's getting really good at that. I bet you win that prize." He got off his bike, leaned it against the porch, and went over to stroke Molly's head.

"I hope so. Georgia holding the little Dot should help." Rachel went over to sit on the porch and set the puppies out of the box onto the porch. She picked one up. Stewart went to sit beside her.

He picked up a puppy too. "Everything is okay." He sighed deeply and smiled at Rachel. "I don't believe Ms. Gibbs is a witch." Stewart poured out the story about the poltergeist book.

"So?" Rachel shrugged. "I don't see what that proves." Then she put down her puppy and held up her hand. "Wait, it does prove something, but it doesn't disprove the witch theory."

Stewart sighed. Sometimes Rachel got on his nerves. "What do you think it proves?"

Rachel gathered up the puppies and put them back in the box. She didn't say anything until she was standing up. "It proves, dummy, that Martha is in on the whole thing. Don't you remember what she said to Ms. Gibbs? Martha is grateful for something Ms. Gibbs has done for her. Maybe Ms. Gibbs is blackmailing her or maybe Martha traded your dad for some magic Ms. Gibbs did for her. Does Martha have a sick mother or anything?

Well, anyway, Martha knows Ms. Gibbs has bewitched your dad, and she doesn't care!"

Why was Rachel always so unreasonable? Stewart jumped up. "You're crazy, Rachel, really crazy." He stomped off, forgetting all about his bike.

His father was reading the paper in the family room when Stewart got inside. They exchanged greetings. Stewart sat down and turned on the TV, but he didn't even try to find something to watch. After a minute, he took a deep breath, and said, "Dad, if you want to marry Ms. Gibbs, it's fine with me."

Dad put down his paper and looked at Stewart. "That's nice to hear, son. It's good to know you've grown up lately. Time will tell about a wedding."

Stewart had expected a more joyous reaction, but it didn't matter. He felt relaxed and free for the first time in what seemed like ages. He flipped off the TV and wandered to the front of the house. Through the big picture window he saw Rachel walk by. She was probably going to Ham's, probably going to share her crazy idea about Martha. Oh well, Sammi might be right about Rachel. He might be better off if he didn't hang around with her. Besides Rachel could be really aggravating.

"Get your algebra book, son." His dad got up and went into the kitchen to sit at the table. "We're in this algebra thing together," Dad said when Stewart was back. "We're in everything together." Stewart actually enjoyed the algebra lesson. Maybe he could just let go and trust his father.

He went to his room and turned on his computer. "Okay," he wrote to Sammi, "I'm thinking I might hang around with Ham and Rachel less. Taylor's noticed me some. What do I do next?"

Sammi was online, and she began to answer at once. "Surely you've called her. Right?" Stewart admitted he hadn't, and Sammi shot back, "Call her, Stew. Call her right now."

He got out his student directory, looked up Taylor Montgomery's number, and dialed it. It only took two rings for Taylor to answer, but that was long enough for Stewart to get scared. "It's me," he said, "Stewart, Stewart Wright."

"Why sure, Stewart," she said. "Of course, I know your voice."

"Oh, that's great! I mean it's great to talk to you." He said, and because she didn't say anything, he knew he had to come up with something else. "Listen, I just wanted to tell you how sorry I am about missing your party." He hoped she would say something because he couldn't think of another word.

"You're soo sssweet." She dragged the last two words out, and the sound of her voice gave Stewart goose bumps.

"Well, guess I'd better go hit the books and everything."

" 'Bye, Stewart. See you Monday." Stewart put down the phone. He couldn't just sit there quietly. Taylor Montgomery recognized his voice and said she would see him on Monday. Suddenly, he was jumping on his bed, like he had done when he was a little kid. One jump, though, and he knew why he hadn't done it lately. He had to duck his head to keep from hitting the ceiling.

Stewart woke on Monday excited about going to school. He knew Taylor Montgomery would speak to him. It was enough to make him bolt out of bed when the alarm went off. He was ready early. Instead of waiting for Ham as usual, he walked around the corner to meet Ham as he came out of his house.

Ham had been gone all day on Sunday, so Stewart had not talked to him. "Come on let's move it," he called to Ham. "I'm in a hurry to get to school."

"Why?"

Stewart began to walk. "Well, for one thing, I've got a feeling Taylor Montgomery might be waiting for me," he called over his shoulder.

"Nah, what are you talking about?" Ham caught up with him, and Stewart told him about the conversation.

"Hmm." Ham frowned.

"What?" Stewart demanded.

Ham shrugged, "Oh, I was just thinking how mad Rachel is going to be if you start hanging out with Taylor. Maybe you haven't noticed, but Rachel doesn't like Taylor much."

"Who I hang out with is none of Rachel's business."

"Well, Brad Wilson isn't going to like it either."

Stewart slapped at Ham's shoulder. "Lighten up, Ham Bone. You worry too much."

The first person they saw inside the building was Ms. Gibbs. She came around the corner just as they stepped into the hall. Stewart froze, knowing she was coming toward him. He kept his eyes down, away from her green necklace. She stopped beside him. "Come on down to my room, Stewart. I need to talk to you," she said softly.

Stewart wanted to look for Taylor, but he didn't say so. "Okay." He waited until Ms. Gibbs started away, then fell in behind her.

"See you later," Ham said, and he hurried off in the opposite direction. Suddenly, following her down the hall, Stewart's resolve to trust Ms. Gibbs began to fade.

At the art room door, she stopped and turned back to him. "We'll only be a minute. You'll still have time to talk to your friends before school starts."

This is the right thing to do, he told himself, but he felt shaky as they entered the room. She closed the door after they got inside. Then she walked to the desk and picked up a small bottle. "I'm not sure I told you," she said, "but one of my hobbies is making cosmetics. I've been working on this new cologne for men. Will you try it out for me?" She was pointing the sprayer in his direction.

"I guess so." He didn't feel he really had a choice.

"Just a dab." She was spraying. "This is strong stuff." The scent was nice, not too powerful, but definitely there. She put the cap back on. "There, go find your friends now."

He muttered a sort of combined thank-you and good-bye. "Stew," she called just before he went out. "Let me know if Taylor likes the cologne."

It didn't take long to find out because he almost bumped into Taylor as he left the room. "Stewart," she said, "I was hoping to see you." She wrinkled her nose. "Boy, do you smell nice!"

He could feel his face getting red. "It's too much, huh?"

"No, oh no, not at all. Just right." She stepped toward him, and he actually wanted to move back. He was shocked. He'd never have figured he'd have to work at avoiding a public display of affection with Taylor Montgomery. "Walk me to my locker, okay?" She smiled at him, and her face nearly touched his. He started to move. Her body did not touch his, but he could feel her near him.

Stewart watched Taylor take her books from her locker and waited until she walked away, waving over her shoulder at him before he went to his own locker. He was late for English.

Between first and second period, he searched the crowd in the halls for a glimpse of Taylor and didn't even notice Brad and Jake walking behind him until they were right in front of the girls' restroom. Suddenly, the two boys were on either side of him, and Stewart knew what was going to happen. He tried to run, but Brad's hands jerked him back. Stewart felt himself being lifted between

Brad and Jake. They each had a hand holding one arm and one ankle. "Want to fly, Wart?" Brad asked. "Want to fly into the girls' bathroom?"

Stewart did fly for just a second, hit the floor, and went sliding on his back into the restroom. He shut his eyes, waiting for girls to scream, but the room was quiet. Then a familiar voice spoke. "Stewart," said Rachel in disgust, "Taylor isn't in here, look somewhere else." She stepped around him and went out the door.

Without raising his gaze from the floor, he jumped and ran. Outside the restroom, he slowed only enough to avoid being called down for running in the hall. Still breathing heavily, he slid into science class.

At lunch Rachel didn't even slow down, just walked by without a glance at the table where Stewart and Ham sat. Watching her, Stewart felt surprised to remember how brave she had been at Ms. Gibbs's and how he had felt good when he comforted her. Just then, though, he saw Taylor walking toward a table full of kids. Brad was there with Jake and Taylor's best friend, Madison, along with two other girls and a boy. Stewart put down his piece of pizza and watched her sit down. Someone said something and everyone laughed. He could see Taylor's white teeth as she put back her head and opened her mouth. What would it feel like, he wondered, to be at that other table, the one with the cool kids?

For a long time he watched, saying almost nothing to Ham. Finally, he picked up his pizza again, looked down, and started to eat. It was a surprise to hear her voice. "Stewart." Taylor had come to the other side of his table. She leaned across toward him. "Do you want these?" She held out two big chocolate-chip cookies. "You need your strength for basketball."

"Hey, that's nice of you," he said. She smiled, and then she was gone.

"She's right," said Ham after Taylor walked away. "You're going to need your strength for basketball, and not just for playing even. Look over there." He leaned his head to the right, and Stewart saw Brad Wilson staring at him from his table. "He's going to be waiting for you in the dressing room," said Ham. "Maybe you ought to get sick and go home before last period." He picked up one of the cookies from Stewart's plate and ate it.

Ms. Gibbs stood in the hall just outside the cafeteria. She motioned for Stewart to come over to her. "Well?" She waited, but when Stewart didn't say anything she went on. "How did the cologne go over?"

"Oh, fine, I guess." He nodded. "Fine."

"The thing is, I've added a new ingredient since this morning." She reached out for Stewart's hand and pressed a small bottle into it. "Put some on right before you go to gym class."

"You mean after, right? To make me smell better after I sweat."

She shook her head. "No, no. This is important. Put it on before. Smelling good will give you confidence while you play. It might even make people feel more friendly toward you."

"Okay." He couldn't think of anything else to say, and he stepped backward to get away from her.

"Use my cologne and you never need worry about being Wart again."

"That's nice. Thank you." After a few steps and a little wave, he turned and almost ran.

"She means Brad," Ham said when Stewart told him about the conversation. "The stuff casts a spell, and it'll protect you from Brad."

They were in front of their lockers, and Stewart jerked hard on the door of his. "I'm dropping the witch business. Remember? My dad is going to marry the woman. She can't be a witch! Quit talking about it and just close your big mouth for once in your life."

"Well, you try to believe that if you want to, but Rachel and I, we know the truth. You'd better spray yourself good with that stuff before you go down into that dressing room." Ham picked up his book and, without waiting for Stewart, walked toward class.

Stewart knew he had been rotten to Ham, and he wondered if Ham would wait for him before gym class, but there he was at his locker as usual. It was best to act normal. "Hey, what's up?"

Ham shrugged, "Just hanging, waiting for you." They walked together toward the gym. Before they went down the steps to the dressing room, Ham grabbed Stewart's arm. "Take out that stuff, and spray yourself. I'm telling you."

"Okay, okay, but it isn't magic." Stewart took the bottle from his pocket and sprayed.

Sure enough Brad was already in the dressing room when they got there. Stewart barely glanced his way, but it was clear from the look on Brad's face that he was furious. Ignore him, Stewart told himself and he bent to untie his shoes. When he raised his head, Brad was there in front of him.

"Stay away from Taylor." Brad grabbed Stewart's shirt, yanked him up from the bench, and pulled him close. Brad's nose began to twitch. "What's that smell?" His voice became calmer, and he let go of Stewart's shirt.

"Let's take it easy," Stewart tried not to let his voice shake. "Hey," Stewart was thinking hard. "If a girl doesn't want you, you sure don't need her. Right?"

Brad chewed for a second at his lip. "Well . . . there's a whole gang of girls who have the hots for me."

"Why sure," Stewart said. "No need to fight over a girl. They're everywhere." He reached out and gave Brad's shoulder a friendly little punch.

"It's the cologne," said Ham when Brad had moved away. "Hang on to that bottle."

It was true that Stewart seemed magic again as they practiced. Every ball he put up found its home in the hoop, and he killed them on defense, too, taking away the ball and moving with it toward his team's goal.

"Son," said Coach Knox after practice. "What is it

with you? We all have our better days, but you're like two different players. We've got to figure what it is that makes you so hot on some days."

Stewart gave the coach a sort of shrug and walked on, but Ham was right behind him. "We know what it is," he said. "Witch power!"

"It is not." Stewart swallowed hard, afraid he might cry. "It just can't be."

· EIGHT ·

On Tuesday the Rams played the Bulldogs, from a neighboring town. "Now, Wright, this is your chance to start," the coach said to Stewart before the game. "Show us you can deliver in the real thing like you've been doing in practice." Walking across the court, Stewart felt good. He made his first shot. The second one missed, but all his others swished through clean and beautiful. Just before halftime, the score was twenty-three to twelve in favor of the Rams, and eighteen of those points belonged to Stewart. He could hear the cheerleaders chanting his name.

When the buzzer sounded, the team headed down toward the locker room. Ham caught up to Stewart on the stairs and followed him to his locker. "Hey," Ham said when Stewart opened the door, "you got that spray in here?" He reached for the bag.

"Sure." Stewart pulled his bag away and stuffed it

back in the locker. "It always makes a person feel more confident if he doesn't stink." He turned his back and began to do some stretching exercises.

"Come off it." Ham moved around Stewart so they were facing each other. "The stuff is magic, and you know it. What I want to know is are you going to share it with me?"

Stewart stared at him. "You just can't admit that I'm becoming a great player." Maybe he'd really be better off without Ham.

Ham made a snorting sound. "Sure you are. Sure you are." He gave Stewart an angry look. "So what will it hurt to spray me?"

"Okay, okay!" Stewart grabbed up the bag, took out the bottle, and shot the stuff all over him.

"Pew," someone yelled. "Enough of that stuff. You're polluting the air!" Stewart walked to the back of the dressing room to join Brad and Jake.

"All right," said the coach when the team went back out after half time, "let's make some substitutions." Everyone knew the team was far enough ahead so that the coach would let some of the second-string guys play. "Ham, you go in for Wright." The other starting players were taken out too.

Stewart gave Ham's hand the good luck slap. "You've got the magic," Stewart said, but he did not smile.

Right off, Ham dropped the ball. Next time he got his hands on it, one of Henderson's players stole it from him.

He never even got a chance to shoot because he couldn't lose the guy who guarded him. The scoreboard showed that Henderson was gaining.

"Stewart," the cheerleaders yelled. "Put Stewart back in."

Stewart knew the coach wasn't likely to be guided by cheerleaders, but he must have been planning the move anyway because in just a few minutes he motioned for Stewart to come down to talk to him. "Ham," he said to Stewart, meaning who was to be replaced.

When Stewart ran out onto the court, he pointed to Ham. There was no good luck slapping of hands. Stewart did not try to hide his sarcastic look.

After the game, the team gathered around Stewart, congratulating him and celebrating their victory. Brad even invited Stewart to go out for pizza with him and Jake.

Ham sat alone on the end of a locker room bench. His head was down, and he looked miserable. Stewart was ready to be friends again. He walked over to Ham and flipped his towel against Ham's shoulder. "So, I guess you know now it isn't the spray, huh?"

Ham looked up. "No," he said, "I still believe the spray is magic, but I know now it's magic just for you, your special formula. But you know what, Wart, I feel sorry for you. You want to be a good basketball player, and you want to be popular. You want those thing so bad you don't care how you get them." He shook his head.

"Hope you have someone to pick you up when it's all over." He shrugged. "But it won't be me, man. I won't be picking you up."

"You're a poor sport, Hamilton," Stewart said. "You can't stand to see me winning." Ham stood up then and walked out of the dressing room without even saying "See you."

At home that evening, he sent Sammi an e-mail. "Okay, I've done it. I probably won't be hanging around Ham and Rachel much in the future."

Sammi fired back, "Great! You're on your way to being popular! Life is going to be fun, Cuz!"

Stewart stared at the words. It was true, he was on his way. He wished he felt better. From that day, life for Stewart was different. Ham no longer came around the corner to walk to school with him. On the first day, Stewart waited for quite a while, just in case. Then realizing Ham must have cut through the other way, he walked alone. At school, he looked up as he passed the library and through the glass walls he saw Ham and Rachel sitting together at a table. Probably studying witchcraft, Stewart thought, and he wished he could throw something at them.

The next couple of weeks, he spent lots of time with Brad and Jake, and at lunchtime, he ate with them and Taylor at the cool table. He told himself that he didn't believe the business about the cologne, but he was never without it either. When his supply ran low, he went to

Ms. Gibbs's room. "I'm not out," he said, "but I . . . you know, don't want to take any chance."

"Oh no, you don't want to run out of this." She reached into the bottom drawer of her desk and pulled out a large bottle. "I won't be here much longer teaching. You will have to be sure to replenish your supply at home."

"Not here?" Stewart took the bottle from her. "Why won't you be teaching?"

She sighed. "Oh, I don't know, this job is hard work. I may look for something easier. Of course after your father and I are married, I'll probably want to stay home, at least for a while." She closed the desk drawer. "Maybe Mr. Harrison will be coming back soon."

In the hall, Stewart moved slowly. Ms. Gibbs's words kept going through his mind. "After your father and I are married." What's wrong with you, he asked himself? You knew they were going to get married. You even told Dad it was okay with you. Still, he hardly had the strength to walk.

The girls' restroom was across and just down the hall from the art room. Stewart looked up to see Rachel coming out of the door. He did not expect her to walk over to him, but she did.

"You," she said, and her face showed her disgust, "have a right to know what I just observed."

Stewart knew Rachel was about to say something unpleasant. He considered walking on, but he knew that

Rachel wouldn't let him get away. "I guess you're going to tell me?" he said.

"I certainly am. That is, if I can get it out without throwing up." Rachel moved to lean against the wall. A sort of shudder passed over her. "Taylor! I just saw your dream girl, Taylor, in the restroom." She looked at Stewart with an expectant expression, but when he didn't say anything, she went on. "She was in there practicing. Looking in the mirror, peering back over her shoulder to see if her rear swayed just right when she walked."

Stewart didn't know what to say. He hadn't had any experience with girls or their rears. "So, you think that's bad?"

"*Think* that's bad!" Rachel's voice was loud, and Stewart looked around, relieved that no one seemed to be paying attention. Rachel's face had turned red, and for a minute Stewart thought she might tear into him with her fists like she had done once when they were little. She didn't hit him, though, not with her hands. "You make me sick," she said really low and mean this time. "You both make me sick, you and your rear-shaking girl-friend."

"She's not exactly my girlfriend," Stewart said weakly.

"She will be if the witch's cologne keeps working."

Now it was Stewart's turn to get angry. "Drop the witch stuff. My Dad and Ms. Gibbs are getting married."

"Okay, believe it isn't the cologne then, if you want to." Her face was twisted with anger. "If it isn't the cologne, it's because you're suddenly such a hotshot ball player. Why would you want a girl who never looked at you when you were just plain Stewart? I used to think you were pretty smart." She stomped away leaving Stewart thinking it might have been easier if she had just hit him with her fists.

That evening he walked home slowly, thinking about how Ham and Rachel were both mad at him. Rachel was already home and playing with the puppies on her front porch. She did not wave at Stewart when he walked by, just pretended she saw no one.

He and Rachel had had arguments before, but he could not remember a time when they didn't speak to each other. It was true he didn't want to hang around with Rachel at school, but not even speaking was too strange. Stewart felt miserable. Maybe he would go in, get Georgia, and go over to Rachel's house. Rachel liked Georgia. She would talk to Georgia, and she wouldn't be hateful to Stewart in front of his little sister. Maybe while they were there he could think of a way to get Rachel to be his friend again.

Georgia was watching TV in the family room. "Want to go over to Rachel's and look at the puppies. They're just about big enough for us to bring one home."

Georgia didn't move, and Stewart tried again. "Rachel's got the puppies out. Let's go."

"I'm not getting a puppy, and I don't want to play with them anymore." Georgia did not take her gaze from the TV.

"You aren't getting one? Why? Who said?" He went to sit beside her on the couch.

"Wanda doesn't like dogs. She says they're smelly and don't make good pets. She knows some people who have special kittens, and she's going to get one for me."

He reached out, put his hands on either side of her face, and forced her to look at him. "Why? You've been planning to get one of the Dots for a long time. You don't have to change your mind because someone else doesn't like dogs."

"I want a kitty," Georgia said. She pulled herself away from him and folded her arms across her chest.

There was another surprise after his father came home. Stewart went into the kitchen, planning to talk to Dad about the puppy thing, but he forgot it when his father made an announcement.

"Today was Wanda's last day at your school." Dad was at the stove dishing up chili for supper. "She just called and said Mr. Harrison will be back tomorrow."

Stewart reached for his bowl, but he felt odd, like he might not be able to hold it. It's almost like the idea just came to her today that she wanted Mr. Harrison well, and now he is well enough to return.

"Oh boy," squealed Georgia. "Wanda can stop being a teacher and be our mommy!"

Stewart looked at his dad, expecting a comment, but he said nothing, just put Georgia's chili on the table, leaned down, and gave her a little hug.

Stewart tried to laugh. "Man, Mr. Harrison got over his crack-up sooner than I thought he would. He seemed pretty far gone, and now just the day Ms. Gibbs tells me she's tired of teaching, Harrison recovers. It's kind of funny, don't you think?"

Dad sat down to eat. "Oh, not so strange. I guess they can do a lot for mental breakdowns with medicine these days." He smiled. "Wanda talked to him herself. He told her they had asked him to stay on at the hospital to teach art to disturbed patients. He claimed he turned them down because it was so dull and normal at the hospital. He prefers the really crazy atmosphere at the middle school."

Georgia and Dad went on talking about Wanda and how now she would have more time to spend on the big Thanksgiving dinner she was planning to cook for them all. "I'll put up the pictures of Pilgrims and Indians," said Georgia, "and make a turkey centerpiece."

Stewart could see that his sister was getting excited. Last year Martha had taken her shopping for little Thanksgiving cutouts for decorations and shown her how to make a turkey from a brown bag.

Dad held out his hand in a *stop* motion. "Now, wait a minute. We've got plenty of time, Thanksgiving is still a week and a half away. Wanda is planning to cook at her house. Let's let her get in on the decorating plans."

"No!" Georgia jumped up and stomped her foot. "We have Thanksgiving at home."

Dad had always made a big deal of having holidays at home. Stewart thought it was because their mother was dead that his dad worked a little harder to give Georgia and him a sense of tradition. The idea of having Thanksgiving dinner at Wanda's didn't appeal to him much either. He felt glad that Georgia would pitch a big enough fit to put a stop to it.

"No!" Georgia said again. She sat back down then and began to eat, but the determined look did not leave her face.

Later Stewart brought up the subject. Georgia had gone upstairs, and Stewart and his father were cleaning up the kitchen. "Guess Wanda won't mind cooking over here when she finds out how important it is to Georgia. Will she?"

Dad shook his head. "No, problem. Wanda will talk to her and change Georgia's mind. Haven't you noticed how marvelous Wanda is with her? She can get that little girl to do anything. It's one of the things I like about the woman."

Stewart felt weak, and he sank into a kitchen chair. It was true! Stewart hadn't thought about it, hadn't even really seen it, but it was true. Wanda Gibbs could handle Georgia like a charm. Dad thought it was Wanda's wonderful way with children, but Stewart did not believe it. The whole thing made him feel sick. Wanda Gibbs was changing his little sister's personality, and Stewart didn't like it.

In a sort of a daze, he climbed the stairs. He wanted to talk this over with Ham or Rachel. He'd try Rachel. Maybe she had gotten some of her anger out of her system when she yelled at him earlier. He took the phone, and slid down the bed to sit on the floor.

"Ms. Gibbs won't be the art teacher tomorrow," he said quickly when Rachel said hello. He thought that piece of information might be interesting enough to keep her from hanging up on him. "Mr. Harrison is coming back."

"Oh yeah?"

"Ms. Gibbs told me today she was getting tired of teaching and maybe Mr. Harrison would come back, almost like it was her idea for him to be well. Besides that, listen, Rachel, the woman has been messing with Georgia's personality, changing her. I don't like that, not Georgia. She'll do anything the woman suggests and—"

"Stewart," Rachel broke in, "are you saying you finally believe Ms. Gibbs is a witch?"

"Georgia even changed her mind about the puppy because Ms. Gibbs said dogs are smelly and make too much noise."

"She did? She really talked Georgia out of taking one of the Dots?" Rachel's tone was unbelieving.

"Easy as pie."

"Well, that should settle it for you all right. Georgia would never give up the puppy, not on her own. Oh, you know something? I've always heard witches don't like dogs because dogs know about them."

"I don't know," he said, "I just can't make up my mind about her. It seems crazy to believe she could really be a witch."

"Well, of course, there's Taylor to consider too."

"What does Taylor have to do with this conversation?" he snapped, and then he was sorry for his tone. He didn't want to make Rachel mad again.

Her voice was gentle though. "Stewart, don't you see she has everything to do with it. If you admit Ms. Gibbs is a witch, you'll have to give up Taylor and being a basketball star. If you decide your little sister is more important than basketball or a girl who knows how to wiggle her bottom, let me know." She put the receiver down without saying good-bye.

·NINE·

At school the next morning, Stewart went first to the art room. Mr. Harrison was in there. Stewart stood in the doorway and called, "I'm glad you're back." Mr. Harrison looked up and smiled. Stewart stayed just a second, looking in. He liked the art room without Ms. Gibbs. Was it his imagination, or was there something different in the air without her? Would that Wanda Gibbs atmosphere soon be in his own home? He gave himself a little shake and moved on.

Things were back to normal in the art room, but not in the rest of his life. From the beginning, each day was wrong. He missed walking with Ham. They'd traveled to school together since kindergarten first in one or the other parent's car and then, when they were bigger, on foot. Now Stewart looked down a lot as he walked, and the three blocks seemed more like three miles.

At school, he did like being part of the popular gang. It was fun to know that even Sammi would approve of the way seats got saved for him at lunch by the "right" people. Kids treated him differently, he thought, now that he hung out with Brad and Jake and got waved at and smiled at by Taylor.

Most of the time Stewart enjoyed being one of the popular group. Sometimes, though, he'd look up and see Ham, all alone in the gym or talking to no one between classes. Well, Ham had brought it all on himself, and Rachel too. They had turned their backs on him, but still he couldn't shake the little cloud of depression that would occasionally hover over him. Once, his depression changed to guilt.

It was between geography and algebra. As usual, Stewart went to his locker, got his books, and hurried to Brad's locker, where they hung out. Brad gathered his books while Jake and Stewart stood beside him on duty. "Girl Watch," the boys called it. They were supposed to make comments about passing girls. Stewart hoped he would get better at coming up with good remarks. Right now his job was mostly just to laugh when Brad or Jake said anything that was meant to be funny, even if it wasn't. He stood there ready to laugh and realized that the girl walking by was Rachel. "Oh look." Jake jabbed Stewart in the ribs and pointed to Rachel's back. "We call that one 'Turnpike.' "

A sour kind of taste came up from Stewart's stomach into his throat. "Turnpike? Why?"

Jake laughed. "Come off it, Wright. Surely you've noticed."

"Noticed?" Stewart shook his head. "Noticed what?"

"No curves," said Brad, "just one long, straight road." Brad closed his locker and moved his hand in a straight up and down line. "Not even a little bump."

"Oh yeah, sure," said Stewart. He tried to smile, but it didn't feel good. He didn't feel good later either. When he looked out his bedroom window that evening just before dark, he saw Rachel on her back porch with Molly and the little Dots. There wasn't enough light to see Rachel's face or her body really well, but Stewart didn't need to see. He knew Rachel. "It was a joke," he whispered. "No one really meant anything mean by it," but when he turned away from the window, he felt the need to talk to someone. Sammi hadn't been e-mailing him lately. Maybe he would have to call her. He wandered downstairs.

His father was watching the news on TV. Stewart stood for a minute, considering talking to his father about how he felt, but the idea made him uncomfortable. Dad didn't like discussions anymore than Stewart did, not about important things. He had enrolled Stewart in a special sex education class at school. Later, on the way home, Dad had started the car and asked, "Any questions?" Stewart could see the relief on his father's face when he shook his head no.

Stewart shifted his weight from one foot to the other. Dad looked at him. "Need something, Stew?"

"Nah," he said. "I was just thinking maybe I'd give

Sammi a call. I mean you wouldn't mind, would you, on account of it being long distance or anything?"

His father turned down the TV and waved toward the phone. "Sure," he said, "go ahead. I'll talk to Susan when you're finished."

Stewart turned away before he answered. "No, Dad, I sort of thought I'd talk to Sammi upstairs."

In his room, Stewart stretched out on the floor with the phone, got the number from the book he had carried upstairs with him, and dialed. He did not make small talk when Sammi answered. Stewart had never particularly enjoyed talking on the phone, and he did not make small talk, ever. "Sammi," he said, "why does it matter what a person looks like? To be popular I mean. I don't see why it matters so much."

"Stew," said Sammi. "I can't answer that question. It's like asking why the sky is blue. No, I'll bet there is some kind of reason you could look up about the sky, but not about how people look. People like people who are nice-looking. It's just a fact, that's all. Lots of people don't care what's inside a person, just how they look. It's a shame, but it's true. What's going on?"

"Nothing." Stewart wanted to hang up. The phone call had been a bad idea.

"Don't tell me nothing," said Sammi. "You never call me. This is maybe like the second time in your whole life."

"I'm just trying to understand the popular thing, that's all."

"Yeah, well, I've got something to tell you about that." Sammi's voice sounded different, and Stewart waited uncomfortably. "I've been thinking about telling you for a while. I'm not so sure anymore about being popular, about it being important."

"What do you mean?" Stewart stood up. Out his window he could still see Rachel.

"I've gotten all involved with the drama club this year. We're doing a great play, and I love my part. Well, there are some great kids in the club, and some of them don't even care about being popular. They just care about drama and getting good parts and giving great performances."

"So are you saying you aren't popular anymore?"

"No, I'm not saying that. I still mostly run around with my same crowd, but I don't know . . . there are different ways of fitting in, I guess." She paused for a minute, and Stewart walked over to lean against the windowsill. "I just don't want to tell you what to do anymore about your friends and stuff. Maybe you don't want to be popular. I'm sorry for pushing you."

Stewart swallowed hard and stared through his window at Rachel. "It's okay, Sammi. I'm glad you told me to be popular. See I really like Taylor. I think she likes me, too, but I'm not sure."

"Well then, I will tell you one more thing. You ought to let her know. Girls like to be told. That's something I can say for sure."

After he hung up the phone, Stewart sat thinking. He did not think about what Sammi had said about popularity not being important. He did not want to go over any of that. He thought only about how Sammi had said he should tell Taylor that he liked her. He had been hanging around with her crowd for almost three weeks, but nothing had happened between him and Taylor. He wanted something more than just sitting at the same table for lunch.

Finally, he reached for his notebook, took a piece of paper, and wrote, "Taylor, will you be my girlfriend? I think you are beautiful. Stewart Wright." His hand shook as he wrote. His hand shook, too, the next day when he opened her locker and slid the note partway into the geography book that lay at the top.

All through first period, he felt uneasy. Maybe Taylor would laugh at him. Taylor laughed at lots of things. He tried to concentrate on all the times she had waved at him and smiled at him with her beautiful lips. She would say yes, she had to. When he came out of the English class, he saw her coming toward him.

"Hi, Stew," she said. "I read your note, and the answer is yes."

Stewart wanted to say something impressive, but all he could come up with was, "Good."

"I'll save you a place beside me at lunch." She walked away then, and Stewart watched her.

Sure enough, when Stewart got his lunch tray and headed toward the popular table, the place beside Taylor was empty. "Hey everybody," she said when he was just close enough to hear, "Stew and I are together now."

Grinning, he slid in beside her. He was sitting beside Taylor when her best friend, Madison, came and sat on the other side of him. Before he had always had one of the boys on at least one side of him, and he squirmed a little on the bench. A joke, he told himself. Make a joke, and one came to him. "Wow," he said, "I get to eat between the presidents!"

The girls both stared at him. "Presidents of what?" asked Taylor.

"Of the United States of America. Madison was number four and Taylor was," he stopped to think, "number twelve, I believe."

"You're strange, Stewart Wright," Madison said. She turned to Taylor. "Isn't he just too weird?"

Taylor smiled at him. "He is, but he's cute too." She put out her hand and touched his face. "Just as cute as he can be."

Stewart could feel his face turning red. What could he say now? In a second, though, he realized it wasn't necessary to say anything. Rachel's friend Ashley walked by, and Madison drew in her breath with surprise. "Look," she said. "Can you believe it?"

"I can't." Taylor rolled her eyes.

"What?" said Stewart. He couldn't see anything shocking about Ashley Sage.

"Her shirt," said Taylor. "She's already worn that same one once this week." She turned to Madison. "Was it Monday?"

"No." Madison made a face. "Tuesday, two days ago. I promise."

"Just look at her. I'd die first," said Taylor.

Stewart did look at Ashley, and he thought her shirt was nice. He watched Ashley go over and sit with Rachel and Ham. The thought came to him that he wished he was at that table, but he pushed it down. After all, there he was beside the girl of his dreams. He decided not to listen, just look. Taylor had on a blue sweater, and it fit her just right. Sometimes she leaned against Stewart, not long enough to get them into trouble, but long enough to make him tingle all over.

The next day they had their third basketball game, and the coach was really excited. "We've won one and lost one," he told the boys that day as they warmed up. "Let's make it two wins for the Rams!"

"Got your spray?" Ham asked Stewart in the dressing room, but he didn't wait for an answer, just moved away from Stewart to get dressed at the other end. Stewart did have his spray. Leave it off, he told himself. Prove it isn't the spray that makes you play well, but he didn't leave it off. He scored sixteen of the twenty-six points that made the Rams victorious.

After the game, Stewart had plans again to join Brad, Jake, and a couple of other boys for pizza. Brad's parents were driving, and Stewart thought he'd better remind his father, who had already given his permission. He found him in the concession stand with a bag of popcorn.

"Oh yeah, right." Dad had popcorn in his hand, but he didn't put it in his mouth. A questioning look on his father's face made Stewart a little uncomfortable. "Is Ham going?"

"No, I don't think so. Why?" Stewart started to step away. "Dad, Ham doesn't have to everywhere I go." He moved away before his father could answer.

With Ms. Gibbs not at school, Stewart was usually able to push worries about her out of his mind. His father continued to see her often, but most of the time Stewart was able to avoid her. He tried to keep his thoughts only on Taylor, but occasionally there was no avoiding the Gibbs issue.

"I've got play tickets," Dad said when Stewart came downstairs on the Saturday morning before Thanksgiving. "It's over in Tulsa, a play Wanda really wants to see. Martha was supposed to babysit Ozgood and Georgia, but she just called. She's got the flu."

"Ah, Dad, I was thinking I'd meet some of the gang at the movies." Stewart dropped on the couch and buried his face in a sofa pillow.

"Look at me, Stewart," his father said.

Stewart opened one eye and turned it toward where his father sat across the room in his recliner. "Dad—"

"You've hardly seen Wanda or Ozgood the last couple of weeks. You told me you were fine with the relationship, remember?"

"I don't have a choice, do I? I mean about the babysitting thing."

"Not really."

"Can we at least do it here? I'd rather be here."

"Wanda said either way would be fine. Thanks, Stew." His father went back to watching the morning news.

Stewart groaned. He'd be trading a chance to sit beside Taylor at the movie for an evening of dealing with Ozgood.

Ms. Gibbs, Ozgood in tow, arrived with pizza and in a joyous mood. "It's so sweet of you to volunteer for babysitting," she told Stewart, and she pinched his cheek. He tried to give his father a dirty look, but Dad kept his eyes turned away.

"Ozgood," Ms. Gibbs said when she kissed him good-bye, "don't forget the rules."

"I won't," he said, but he seemed sad and suddenly small.

Stewart reached out to put an arm around him. "We'll have a good time, won't we, buddy?" He determined he would get Ozgood involved in some kind of game. Georgia had her ponies spread out across the floor. "We'll find something fun to do," Stewart told Ozgood. They had shelves full of different games, but before Stewart could even open the closet, Ozgood walked to the back door and looked out.

"Is it permissible for me to go into the yard?" he asked.

"Sure." Stewart turned toward him. "I'll go with you."

Ozgood opened the door. "I prefer to be alone if you do not mind."

"Okay." Stewart wandered into the sunroom. He could see Ozgood, sitting on the kitchen steps. Despite what he had told his father, the idea of having Wanda Gibbs as a stepmother still made Stewart uncomfortable, but watching Ozgood, he did feel real affection for the strange boy.

Then Stewart saw something that amazed him. A small rabbit hopped from beneath the porch. Stewart had seen the creature earlier in the yard. It had seen him, too, and had run away. Stewart hadn't known it had found a safe resting place under the porch. Now it moved slowly toward Ozgood, who held out his hand and said something to the animal. The little wild rabbit came directly to stop at Ozgood's feet and stayed still while the boy stroked it. Stewart watched until Ozgood straightened, and the rabbit moved on.

"I'm going outside," Stewart called to Georgia who played in the next room. He pushed open the patio doors, stepped outside, and moved toward the back porch.

"Wow," he said to Ozgood. "I saw the rabbit. That's incredible!"

Ozgood shrugged. "Not really. Animals like me, that's all. His name is Henry." Ozgood stood up. "I'd like to go inside and draw his picture if you have paper."

Stewart had paper, a big drawing pad he had bought for art class and never used. For most of the evening, he and Georgia watched Ozgood draw. He drew Henry in a garden, Henry hopping across the yard, and Henry with his family. "This is Albert, and this one is Wilson," Ozgood said. "They're his brothers. He told me about them."

"How'd you learn to draw like this?" Stewart asked.

Ozgood looked up from his paper. "Mother taught me some." He smiled. "Mostly I just know."

"Does your teacher put your pictures on the bulletin board for best work?" Georgia asked.

"I am homeschooled," said Ozgood. "Mother teaches me, and a friend of hers filled in while she worked at your school. People don't see my pictures much."

"Well," said Stewart. "People are going to see them now. Can we keep one of these, the one with Henry and his brothers? I'm going to get a frame for it, and we'll hang it right here in the family room."

"I'll give one to Martha too," said Ozgood. "She loves my pictures."

"Ozgood," said Stewart. "Do you know why you and your mother moved here?"

Ozgood did not look up. "Mother came to help Martha," he said.

< 164 >

"Help Martha with what?"

Ozgood shook his head. "I don't think I ever knew what help Martha required."

Ozgood fell asleep that night on the couch. Georgia had gone up to her bed. Stewart was sleepy, but he did not go up to bed. He stayed near Ozgood and watched an old movie on TV until his Dad and Wanda came home. Dad gathered up Ozgood to carry him to the car. Stewart handed the other pictures to Ms. Gibbs, but he kept the one of the three rabbits.

Life for Stewart was good. He was at the top of his game every day in gym. There was no game the week of Thanksgiving. They wouldn't play again until the first week in December. He knew he would start and he would play well. Taylor Montgomery was his girlfriend, and everyone in the school knew it.

On the Monday before Thanksgiving, Stewart was just getting home and about to go in his front door when he heard Rachel call his name. She hadn't spoken to him in weeks, but he turned to see her coming toward him. She had a puppy in her arms. "It's the last little Dot," she said. "I sold the other three. I just wish Georgia would take her before someone else does. Molly won't ever have any other puppies."

"Yeah, I know." Stewart did not like discussing Georgia's change of mind concerning the puppy. "It's not up to me, though."

Rachel moved closer. "What is up to you, Stewart? Do

you take responsibility for anything?" She didn't wait for an answer, but he could see the disgust on her face. "Will Ms. Gibbs let Georgia go through with helping me at the pet show?"

Stewart could feel his neck getting hot, soon his face would be red. "Well," he said, "I don't know for sure."

For a long minute, Rachel looked at him. Then without another word she turned and walked back toward her house.

On Tuesday he learned that Thanksgiving dinner was to be at Ms. Gibbs's house. "I thought you really wanted to have Thanksgiving here," Stewart said to Georgia at dinner after he heard the news.

"Wanda says it doesn't matter where we eat." Georgia stopped to put another bite of baked potato into her mouth. "What matters is that the family is all together."

Stewart stared at his father. How could his father not see that Wanda Gibbs was tampering with Georgia's mind? Had the woman truly bewitched his father? It was something he tried not to think about. "I'm not very hungry," Stewart said, and he pushed himself back from the table.

Just as planned, Thanksgiving was at Ms. Gibbs's house. Stewart tried to enjoy the day. Wonderful smells did reach his nose the moment Georgia opened the door for them. Dad had dropped Georgia off early with her decorations. Last year's paper bag turkey sat in an honored place in the center of the table, but Stewart thought its feathers sagged more than when Georgia had first taken it out this year.

"Look what Wanda made for me." Georgia ran to get a dress that hung over the back of a chair. It was made of a pink shiny material and had lots of ribbons. She held it up to her and twirled. "Isn't it beautiful?"

"It is," said Dad. "You will look like a princess."

"It's for the wedding," Georgia said, "for when we get a new mommy."

"Oh," said Dad, and he smiled. Stewart did not smile. He could not smile. He turned away to look at the table.

Dad went on into the kitchen to greet Wanda, but Stewart stayed in the dining area. Wait, he thought, there are only four plates laid out on the table. Stewart looked again. Yes, there were only four. Stewart glanced up to see Wanda Gibbs in the kitchen doorway, watching him.

"Ozgood won't be with us," she said. "He's visiting friends."

A shiver passed over Stewart. Hadn't Ozgood said he didn't have any friends? "Didn't you tell Georgia the important thing about Thanksgiving was having the family all together?"

Wanda gazed at Stewart, and her eyes seemed to narrow, but before she said anything, Dad stepped out of the kitchen. "Stew," he said, "let Wanda manage her son."

< 167 >

Stewart shrugged. "Sure," he said. In his mind he added, sure let her manage Georgia too. Maybe that suits you, Dad, but it does not suit me. He decided to bring up the pet show right in front of Wanda. A few minutes into the meal he put down his fork. "Georgia, I was talking to Rachel about the show at the Pet Place tomorrow. You're still planning to help her with Molly Dot, aren't you?"

Georgia glanced at Wanda Gibbs. "Oh," she said, "I love pet shows. Molly can do the best tricks, and I can hold a little Dot."

Stewart pretended to be interested in spreading butter on a roll. "There's only one Dot left. Rachel's sold the other three."

"She has?" Georgia frowned.

"Georgia doesn't want a dog, Stewart. I am going to get her a special cat. One of my friends has a cat with some darling kittens. As soon as they are old enough, I'll get one for Georgia."

"But you could still help Rachel with the pet show. Remember how we decided having you hold one of the little Dots would be so cute?"

"It wouldn't hurt to help with the show, would it?" Georgia looked at Wanda.

"Of course, it wouldn't hurt." James Wright spoke up. "You don't want to let Rachel down."

"That's right," said Stewart.

Wanda Gibbs stood up. "You know what?" she said.

"I forgot to tell you about what I have upstairs. It's a wonderful creature that I am sort of babysitting for a friend. You could take it to the Pet Place and win your own prize. No need to be just a helper in the contest."

"What is it?" Georgia's eyes were big.

"Hey," said Stewart, "what about Rachel?" He turned to look at his father. "Dad, remember what you said about not letting down Rachel?"

"Oh," Dad said, "you could still help Rachel, and have your own entry."

Stewart could feel Wanda's eyes on them. He could tell that she didn't want Georgia to help Rachel.

"Why don't you all just finish your meal," said Wanda, "and I'll go upstairs and bring it down." She turned back to the antique china cabinet behind her, picked up a plastic cake carrier that sat there, and headed upstairs. "You're going to love this pet," she called out just before she started up the stairs.

Stewart stared down at his plate. "Oh goody, a surprise," said Georgia. "I love surprises." She reached over to pull at Stewart's sleeve. "What do you think it is? Maybe it's a pony."

"Wanda wouldn't keep a pony upstairs," said their father.

Stewart didn't say a word, but he knew. He knew what Wanda kept upstairs, and he knew that she planned to put that something in the cake carrier. In only a minute or so, Ms. Gibbs came back. She held the cake carrier out in front of her. Stewart noticed there were holes all across the top of the plastic lid. Had they been there earlier? He wondered.

"Where's the surprise?" Georgia asked, and she started to push back her chair.

Wanda held out her hand in a stop gesture. "Wait, now. Stay where you are, and I'll show you." She set the cake carrier back on the china cabinet. "Voilà!" she said, and she took off the lid. There sat a huge green frog. If that's Ozgood, thought Stewart, he's grown since the last time. Maybe Wanda wanted him to be more noticeable. "He does tricks," she said.

Georgia clapped her hands. "Tricks! I love tricks. Show me."

Wanda reached over to the table and pinched off a small piece of roll. She held up the piece of bread, and snapped her fingers. The frog jumped up high, took the bread from her hand, and landed back on the cake carrier.

Dad and Georgia laughed. "It's his Thanksgiving dinner," Dad said.

Stewart didn't laugh. He swallowed hard and looked down at the table. Poor Ozgood, a piece of bread was not much of a Thanksgiving feast. Georgia got up and went over to stroke the frog's back. "Can I take him home with me, just for tonight, and take him to the pet show tomorrow?"

Wanda patted Georgia's head. "Oh, I don't think so,

darling. I'd better keep my eye on Froggy. My friend would be really mad at me if something happened to him, but you and your daddy can come by to pick us up for the pet show. I can almost guarantee Froggy will win a prize."

· TEN ·

Stewart didn't sleep well that night. He had a feeling of dread about the next day and about his whole life. "I'm not going to the pet show," he announced at breakfast the next morning.

"Please," said Georgia, but Stewart shook his head. A little later, he stood at the big front window and watched his father and sister head toward the car. On the windowsill was a dead cricket. An idea came flashing into his mind, maybe a way to prove to himself that the frog was or was not Ozgood. He opened the door, and yelled, "Wait for me." Next he ran to the kitchen for a plastic bag.

"Oh, I'm so glad," said Georgia when he got to the car. "I wanted you to see me and Froggy win a prize."

Stewart grunted and got in the front seat. He wasn't going because his little sister wanted him to go. He stared out the car window. So what will you do if you prove to yourself that the frog is Ozgood, he asked himself, but he did not come up with an answer. One step at a time. That's all he could manage. He gave himself a little shake. Do you really want to do this? If Ozgood was a frog, Ms. Gibbs was a witch. If Ms. Gibbs was a witch, Stewart had become popular because of a witch's spell. The car was pulling into Ms. Gibbs's driveway, and Stewart wanted to get out and run. The thought of just chucking it all and running away from home went through his mind.

"Why don't you get in the back, Stew," his father said, "so Wanda can get up front."

"Okay." Stewart opened his door just as his father was getting out. "Ozgood can hop in back with Georgia and me," he said.

"No," said his father, "I don't think Ozgood is home yet."

That's not what I said, Stewart thought, but he got out of the car and climbed into the back. Georgia bounced on the seat when she saw Ms. Gibbs come out of the house with the cake carrier.

"I'll help Rachel," Georgia said, "but I don't want the little Dot." She sighed. "I just had to quit liking dogs after Wanda told me she didn't like them either. They are just too smelly. And they bark way too much."

"And they don't like witches," Stewart muttered.

"What?" said Georgia, but she didn't press the issue.

Wanda had opened the back door to set the cake carrier between Georgia and Stewart.

"When is Ozgood coming home?" Stewart asked when they were driving toward the Pet Place.

Ms. Gibbs turned in her seat to smile at him. "It is so nice of you to be interested in my little boy," she said. "Actually, I'm not certain. Our friends will drop him off sometime today. They have a little boy just Ozgood's age."

Stewart drew in a deep breath and a bit of courage. "Ozgood told me he didn't have any friends," he said.

Ms. Gibbs smiled at him again, but Stewart saw that the smile was on her lips only, not in her eyes. "Stewart, darling," she said, "Ozgood exaggerates a good deal. Haven't you noticed?"

Stewart didn't know what to say, but he wasn't ready to drop the subject. "Well, anyway, I wish he could see the pet show."

"He doesn't care a lot for such things," Ms. Gibbs said. "Ozgood's too serious, you know. I'm afraid it's my fault, somehow."

Even from the backseat, Stewart could see the warm look his father gave Ms. Gibbs. "I think Stewart and Georgia will help him loosen up," he said, and Ms. Gibbs reached over to pat his shoulder.

When the car was stopped in front of the pet store. Georgia reached out for the carrier. "Let me carry Froggy," she said.

"I don't know," said Dad. "He's pretty heavy. Better let Stewart carry him most of the time."

Stewart took the carrier. A line from an old song he had heard ran through his mind, "He ain't heavy. He's my brother."

Pet Place was a huge building. They stopped inside the door and looked around. In a far corner a big circle was roped off for the contest. Rachel was there with Molly on the far side of the ring. She had the puppy in a kind of sling that hung from her neck, and the little dog's head stuck out to see the world. "Oh," said Georgia, "that baby Dot looks so sweet." Stewart saw his sister start to move, and he knew she wanted to run to Rachel. He wasn't surprised when Ms. Gibbs reached for her hand and held her firmly. Georgia didn't pull away.

There were three other dogs, a parakeet, and a white rat with their owners, who sat in folding chairs. The bird and the rat were in cages, and the dogs all had leashes. "There isn't a single cat in the contest, I guess," said Stewart.

"I don't think cats are easy to teach tricks to," said Dad as they moved toward the circle.

"You'd be surprised," said Ms. Gibbs. "I've known some really well-trained cats." That familiar little shiver passed over Stewart.

Georgia slipped under the rope, then reached back to take the cake carrier from Stewart. Ms. Gibbs leaned across the rope to remove the lid. "Stay put until your jump, Froggy," she said, and Stewart thought she sounded as if she believed the frog understood. Dad took a card from a man with a white beard. He wore a Pet Place name tag that said "Carl." Dad wrote Georgia's name and Froggy's on it before he handed it back to the man, who gave each of them a small voting machine. "Just punch for your favorite," Carl said. "I would imagine that will be . . ." He looked at the card, "Froggy." Another employee brought a chair for Georgia, who held the carrier with the frog on it.

Stewart could feel Rachel's stare, but he did not look her way. Carl smiled at Georgia. "Ladies, gentlemen, and children of all ages, we will start with our youngest owner, Georgia Wright and her pet, Froggy. Remember the Pet Place Corporation will award a prize of a hundred dollars to the pet selected by you as the most talented. Only one vote will be recorded by each machine, so don't vote until you've seen all the tricks."

When Ms. Gibbs reached into her purse for the piece of bread, Stewart knew he had to move fast. He pulled the plastic bag from his pocket and took out the cricket. "Let me give him this," he lifted his hand with the insect, but Ms. Gibbs slapped his hand.

"No," she said, "I don't want him eating that!" She handed the piece of bread to Georgia. "Snap, dear," she said.

Georgia held out the bread, snapped her fingers, and the frog jumped for it. The crowd applauded. Georgia smiled, and holding the carrier in front of her, she bowed her head, just as Ms. Gibbs had taught her. Then she handed the carrier to Stewart and slipped out of the ring to stand beside Ms. Gibbs.

Ms. Gibbs turned to put the lid on. "It was good of you to bring the cricket," she said to Stewart, "and of course, most frogs do like bugs. This one, though, is a little different. I didn't mean to be rude, but I was afraid you would give him the cricket before I could explain that Froggy can't eat such things. They make him sick."

Stewart felt frozen, but he managed to nod his head and mumble, "Sure." To him everything seemed dream-like now, and he blinked his eyes trying to focus. The girl with the parakeet took it from its cage, and the green bird sat on her finger. Stewart's heart raced, and the green color of the bird seemed to spread over the girl who held it. The parakeet said, "I love you. I love you. I love you." At least, that is what the announcer said the bird would say. Stewart couldn't understand the parakeet's words. At first, he thought it was probably his condition, but then he was fairly certain he saw doubtful expressions on other faces too.

The boy who owned the white rat held him in his hand. When he released the rat, it ran up the boys arm, across his shoulder, climbed onto the cage, and made its way back inside. "Nothing special, so far," Ms. Gibbs whispered.

The first two dogs to perform both stood on their

back legs to beg for a treat. Then a dog jumped through a hoop. Somehow Stewart focused enough to think that Molly would win. None of the other tricks were as good as Molly's Patty Cake. "Now for the last performer," Carl announced. "Here is Rachel Thomas and her Molly Dot. Her assistant will hold Molly's baby. Rachel handed the puppy to Georgia before she turned back to Molly."

"Sit," Rachel said, and she reached into her pocket for the treat. Later, going over it all in his mind, Stewart remembered that Ms. Gibbs put her arm around Georgia. That, he decided, was the reason for Molly's behavior. Rachel held up the treat and snapped her fingers. Molly didn't sit up. Instead she turned her head to look at Ms. Gibbs. A low growl came from Molly. "Sit," said Rachel again, but Molly did not sit. Molly lunged. She lunged at Ms. Gibbs, who screamed and ran. Molly followed, her leash bouncing after her. "Stop, Molly!" Rachel yelled, but Molly did not stop.

The crowd scattered, a couple of women screamed, and Molly barked. "Stop that animal!" Carl yelled. Suddenly three other dogs were running too. They had broken away from their owners, who were now shouting their names.

For a second, Stewart did nothing except stare. Move, he told himself. He set the cake carrier on one of the chairs inside the ring, and started after Molly. He caught a glimpse of Ms. Gibbs across the big room, her feet pounding the cement floor as she ran toward the door.

Molly was close behind. All at once, Molly stopped, sat down, and howled. Stewart was closer now, and he moved his head from side to side. What had become of Ms. Gibbs? She could not have made it to the door, but she was not in sight. He did not stop running, and he reached Molly before Rachel got there. He grabbed the dog's leash. "Whoa, girl. Stay, Molly."

Then Rachel reached them. She held the puppy in her hands. "See," she said. "I told you. Molly hates her."

"Get that dog out of here!" Carl crossed the floor, waving his hand in a dismissive way. Rachel's mother was right behind him. Stewart still held Molly's leash, but Rachel snatched it from him.

"I'll take her," she said. "You'd better be checking on your witch."

Stewart stood up and looked around. Ms. Gibbs was nowhere to be seen. His father and Georgia came toward him. His father had the carrier under one arm and the lid in one hand. Froggy was not with them. Stewart moved in their direction. "Where's Ozgood?" he said when they were close enough to hear.

"Ozgood?" His father stopped walking and stood beside him.

"I mean the frog." Stewart did not meet his father's gaze. "I mean where's the frog?"

"Someone must have bumped the lid. A lot was happening, and I didn't notice. We need to find him. Wanda will be upset." His father looked around.

"Where is Wanda?" Georgia was crying. "Why did Molly act so mean? Molly is never mean."

Just then a voice came over the store's speaker. "Ladies and gentlemen," Carl said. "I am sorry to announce the pet contest is canceled. Each pet will be awarded a three months' supply of food, and thank you for shopping at the Pet Place."

"Let's go out to the car and see if Wanda is there." Dad started toward the door. "We'll let her decide what to do about the frog."

Georgia had to be pulled along by her father. "Froggy might get stepped on," she wailed.

Stewart saw Rachel, her mother, and Molly about to leave the building. Rachel turned back to look at Stewart just before she went out.

"Wait!" Stewart called. Leaving his father and sister behind, he hurried toward Rachel. She turned away and went out. Stewart waited near the door. He did not want to go on to the car alone. Ms. Gibbs would be furious over the dog attack, and he certainly didn't want to be the person to tell her the frog was missing. Let Dad deal with Wanda Gibbs. Stewart planned to climb into the backseat, hopefully uninvolved.

Dad and Georgia finally came out. Both the lid and the carrier were stuck under Dad's arm now, and he was pulling Georgia behind him. "Come on," he told Stewart. "Get her other hand." They dragged her between them toward the car.

Ms. Gibbs sat in the front seat. At first she faced in the other direction. Stewart wanted to crawl inside before she realized they were there, but Wanda Gibbs whirled around just as they approached the car. Stewart hunched his shoulders and stared at the parking lot pavement.

"It's okay," Georgia's voice sang out. "Wanda's smiling at us. She must have Froggy, else she'd be crying, wouldn't she, Daddy?"

"Let's just get you into the car." Dad reached out and opened the back door. That's when Stewart gasped with surprise. There was Ozgood! He sat in the backseat with his earphones in his ears, and he swayed slowly to what Stewart knew must be his weird music.

"Where'd Ozgood come from?" Dad asked Wanda while he pushed Georgia over to the middle of the backseat.

Georgia didn't wait for the answer. She had her own questions. "Do you know we lost Froggy?"

Wanda turned back to smile at them all. "Don't worry about Froggy. I picked him up on my way out, and the friend he belongs to was just bringing Ozgood in to me. Didn't that work out well?"

Stewart shot a look toward his father. Surely the man wouldn't fall for such a flimsy story. Was his Dad so slow-witted that he couldn't see that Wanda had turned the frog back into the boy?

"Get in, Stewart," was all his father said before closing the back door and going to the front. As he got in, he put out his hand to touch Wanda's cheek. "Are you okay?"

"I'm fine," she said, "but something has to be done about that vicious dog." She shuddered and pulled her sweater closed. "That animal needs to be put to sleep."

"No!" screamed Georgia. "Molly's a good dog. Most usually she is. Please don't make her dead."

Ms. Gibbs turned in her seat. "Oh, darling," she said. "I wasn't serious. We'll just ask the girl to keep her away from us, won't we? Surely even that girl is smart enough to see that the dog needs to be tied up at all times."

"Her name is Rachel," said Stewart. "She wasn't in art, but you've met her. The girl's name is Rachel, and she is smart enough. She's plenty smart."

"Oh yes, your friend. Well, if she's smart enough to keep that dog tied up, everything will be fine, won't it?" Ms. Gibbs flashed her biggest smile toward the backseat.

Stewart leaned back against the seat. Beside him, Georgia was starting to whimper again. "I thought we'd win a prize, but we didn't," she said.

"Well," said Ms. Gibbs, "why don't we go buy a nice Christmas tree and decorate it this evening. It would make us all feel good."

"I'm afraid it's too early," Dad said. "The tree would dry out."

"Oh no," said Ms. Gibbs. "I don't mean a real tree. We'll get a lovely artificial one."

"You mean for your house?" asked Dad.

"I don't think we need two trees, do you? We'll get a tree for your house."

Stewart leaned forward in the seat. "We always get a real tree, right, Dad? We don't like fake trees."

"That's right," said Dad. "It's sort of a family tradition."

"Well," said Wanda, "if we're seriously thinking of becoming a new family, we need new traditions."

"We don't like fake trees," Georgia repeated. "That's because our mommy would never have one. She wouldn't, would she, Daddy?"

The car seemed full of quiet. Wanda had her head turned toward Dad, and Stewart could see that her eyebrows were raised in a questioning expression. Finally, she spoke. "So there can be no artificial tree?"

Stewart couldn't see his father move, but he knew Dad was squirming inside. "Well, kids," he said, "we might rethink this tree thing. They have really improved the artificial ones lately."

"No." Georgia folded her arms across her chest.

Ms. Gibbs turned to look at her. "Georgia, darling," she said, "real trees are so messy, and besides I'd like to decorate one tonight. Wouldn't you?"

"I like real trees," said Georgia.

Stewart did not say a word. Instead he sat, almost unable to breathe. This was, he decided, the final test. He needed one more piece of proof. The outcome of this conversation could make a big difference in his future.

"Do you really like real trees?" asked Wanda. "I've always hated the way they lose their needles, and then the needles get in the rug and stick in your bare feet on Christmas morning."

"I like the same kind of trees you do," said Georgia, and she smiled. Ms. Gibbs reached back to pat her cheek.

"Good," said Ms. Gibbs. "Let's go pick out our tree."

Stewart glanced at Ozgood who had taken the earphones out. The little boy turned his head toward Stewart. "Mother is always victorious," he whispered.

A great rage rose up in Stewart. The woman in the front seat was controlling the mind of his little sister. His father, too, was under a spell. There was no one to stop her, no one except him. He would fight! Stewart squared his shoulders. He was a warrior who could see the enemy about to burn his home with his family inside, but he had to stay calm, had to fight wisely. "Take me by the house first, please," he said, and he thought his voice sounded normal.

"Don't you want to be in on picking out the tree?" Dad asked.

"No," said Stewart, "you guys go ahead. I promised Ham he could come over to watch a movie with me."

"Well, then," said Ms. Gibbs, "let's swing by my place and pick up that apple pie we didn't even cut and some of the leftover turkey. Growing boys need snacks to go with their movies."

While Ms. Gibbs ran inside for the food, Stewart sat

numbly in the backseat, grateful for Georgia's chatter about trees, Christmas, and Santa Claus. "Have fun picking out a tree," he said, when the car pulled into his own driveway.

He walked slowly toward the front door, but when the car was out of sight, he changed directions, heading to Rachel's house. He rang the bell, and Rachel came to the door. "I'm ready to fight her," he said.

·ELEVEN·

What?" said Rachel. The anger in her eyes made Stewart look down at the porch.

"Okay, Rach," he said, "you're right. You've been right all along, and I've been really dumb. I'm sorry." He had the nerve then to look up. "I want to fight. I *have* to fight." He held out both hands, wide from his body with palms up and open. "The thing is, I need help. I need you and Ham."

She folded her arms across her chest and studied him. Neither of them said anything. Stewart wanted to look away, but he didn't. "So, you've come to your senses?" she said finally, and he nodded. Rachel rested her back against the doorframe. "What about Taylor and basketball? If you fight Ms. Gibbs, she might undo her spell."

He shrugged. "If it is a spell, and I'm afraid it is . . ." He tried to smile. "Well, if my success in basketball isn't real, I guess I don't want it."

Rachel leaned her head to one side and raised an eyebrow. "You guess?"

"I know," he said.

"And Taylor?"

"That's an easy one," he said. "I've eaten with the presidents enough." He grinned, and she grinned back. He had known she wouldn't ask, "Presidents of what?"

They went to Stewart's house, where they called Ham, who wasn't very friendly at first or at all interested in coming over. "I'm sorry I've been such a jerk," said Stewart. "I shouldn't have said that stuff about you being jealous and me being tired of you. You're my best friends, you and Rachel. I'm sorry I've ignored you lately."

"Well," said Ham.

"I've got an entire apple pie over here," said Stewart. "And witch or not, the woman can cook."

"No one can think well on an empty stomach," said Ham minutes later, as he stepped inside the house.

"We can't eat down here." Stewart moved to look out the front window. "They could come back any time. I don't want to look up and see that woman coming toward us."

"Me either, not after what Molly did," said Rachel.

They made turkey sandwiches spread with mayo, collected pickles, chips, and soft drinks to fill two trays.

Rachel carried paper cups, plates, and napkins and eating utensils. "I'll come back for the pie," said Ham, and he did as soon as his tray was unloaded on Stewart's desk.

Rachel sat at the desk, Ham on the bed, and Stewart chose the floor, with his back against the door. "This way there won't be any surprises," he said.

"Not unless she can kind of, you know, materialize through things," said Rachel.

"I think that may be what she did at Pet Place," said Stewart, and he shuddered. "I really do. I think she just sort of floated through the door to get away from Molly."

"You guys," said Ham, reaching for a sandwich, "this fight isn't going to be a piece of cake." They looked at each other, and Stewart could feel his friends' resolve, matching his.

Between the sandwiches and the pie, they started a list. "Just say an idea that comes into your mind, anything at all that we might try," said Rachel. She took a piece of paper from a stack on Stewart's desk. "I'll write them down, and we'll go back over them. Even a bad idea might lead to another thought, something we can use."

After an hour, they had eaten most of the pie, but the list was not long. "Read it, Rach," said Stewart. "Like you said, maybe something will click."

Rachel stood. "We have, number one, go to the police." She paused and looked at each boy.

"Nothing," said Ham. "Go on."

"Number two, search the Internet for some sort of

witch-busting outfit." Again she waited. "Number three, ask a priest for advice." No one said anything. "Number four, Stewart could talk to his aunt Susan." She shook her head. "Last, go to the child protective services. It's all we have, guys. Now what?"

"You know what's wrong with that list?" Stewart pushed himself up from the floor and began to pace between the bed and the desk. "Don't you see?" He waved his hands in a gesture of dismissal. "Never mind, I'll tell you. Everything on that list depends on someone else, some outsider who we'd have to convince and then count on for help."

"Not going to happen," said Rachel.

"We are all we've got," said Ham.

Just then Stewart moved toward the window. "I think I hear a car," he said. He lifted the curtain. "They're back. Hurry, Rachel, get down the stairs and out the back door. I don't want her to see you now because of Molly."

Ham jumped off the bed. "I'll go with you," he said, and he grabbed a paper plate with the last piece of pie on it.

Stewart ushered them down the stairs and into the kitchen. He opened the back door, but just before they went out Ham put out his hand, took Stewart's, and put it on top of his own. Rachel joined them in the hand stack. "Go, team!" said Stewart.

"We're all we've got," said Ham, and he ran with Rachel out the back door. Stewart watched, just able to see well enough to know that they both went through the gate that had always connected his yard to Rachel's.

"We'll keep thinking," he heard Rachel shout, and then the front door was opening.

"Stew, come see our new tree," Georgia yelled from the living room. It wasn't, he could see, so much a tree as it was a box, a big box his father and Ms. Gibbs were struggling with on the porch.

"How'd you get this thing in the van?" Stewart asked, and he went to grab one end of the box.

"Had to tie it on." His father was sweating.

"Oh, but it will be worth it. Just wait till you see it all decorated." Wanda held the door while Stew and his father dragged in the box. It took hours to put the tree together, dozens of flat fake branches had to be fluffed out and slipped into color-coded slots.

While Stewart, Dad, Ozgood, and even Georgia worked, Wanda Gibbs flitted about making encouraging comments and calling everyone sweet names. Stewart began to think of excuses to get away. He wanted desperately to go upstairs and be alone. Finally, she said, "Goodness, Jimmy darling, you must be starved. I'll go make sandwiches." No one ever called his father Jimmy. Stewart even remembered having heard his father say he could not tolerate it, even as a boy.

But all he said was. "You've read my mind again, Wanda." Stewart felt sick to his stomach.

"I think I'm about to vomit," Stewart said.

He didn't vomit. In his room he gathered up the trash and leftover food, stuffed it all in a pillowcase, and shoved it in the closet. His dad would be coming up to check on him, and he didn't want to talk about why they had eaten upstairs when he and Ham were supposedly going to be watching a movie downstairs.

He turned off the light and threw himself on his bed. Sure enough, in seconds, Dad knocked and opened the door. "You okay, Son?"

"Just a little queasy." He did not turn toward the door. "I'll be all right."

"Wanda wants to come up. Seems she knows some kind of trick about rubbing your hand to make nausea go away."

Stewart wanted to scream. He'd seen all of the tricks from Wanda Gibbs he could bear to see. "That's nice of her dad, but I just want to sleep."

"Well," said his father, "I'll leave the door open. Just give us a shout if you need something."

Stewart grunted. When his father was gone, he lay in the dark listening. Downstairs they were playing Christmas music and decorating the fake tree. He closed his eyes, and then he sat up straight. Suddenly he knew what he had to do. He slid off his bed, got the phone, and dialed Rachel's number. With his foot he reached out to push the door closed, but still he kept his voice down. "Hi," he said. "I have an idea. I've got—"

"To run away," she said.

He pulled in his breath in surprise. "How'd you know what I was going to say?"

"The same idea came to me. I was just going to call you. It's absolutely the only thing you can do."

"Wow," he said, "the same idea came to us both. Maybe we've got some magic on our side too. Call Ham. We'll plan tomorrow."

The next day, the Saturday after Thanksgiving, was beautiful. They met at the park, not far from their houses. Because it was early, no little kids were there yet, and they pretty much had the place to themselves. No one said, "Let's play first." It just started with Stewart going down the slide.

Rachel was first to run to the monkey bars. "Watch me skin a cat," she yelled like she had when they were eight years old.

They played on the swings too, seeing who could go the highest. Rachel won, but Stewart felt so good, flying high in the sky with his friends. For a few minutes they let themselves soar. Then Stewart began to slow himself down. It was time to plan. They stayed in the swings, barely moving and dragging their feet in the sand.

Finally, the run-away plan was complete. Stewart would shake up his father by disappearing, leaving a note explaining that he could not, after all, accept Wanda Gibbs. Dad would question Rachel and Ham, who would admit they knew where Stewart was, but would refuse to tell until he promised to end things with Ms. Gibbs.

"Your parents are going to insist you tell," said Stewart.

Rachel laughed. "Mine might not. My mother doesn't want your father to marry Wanda Gibbs. She doesn't like seeing the woman come to your house, says she can tell by looking that your mother would hate having her around you and Georgia, and since the episode with Molly, she's even more certain."

"Besides," said Ham. "What can our parents do to us to make us tell? They can have us arrested and put in ju-vie hall if they want to. We aren't snitching." He and Rachel did a high five.

"Thanks, guys," said Stewart, "Thanks for every-thing." His voice shook a little, choked up with tears. He looked down at the sand and changed the subject. "I've got to find out when buses go to Tulsa. I hope I can get one and get there before Dad finds out I'm gone."

"You've got two days to get ready," Ham said. "Do you think Ms. Gibbs will know somehow when she sees you?"

"Wow." Stewart got up from his swing. "I hope not. I won't let myself think about it when she's around."

The next day, Sunday, was easy. Claiming his stomach wasn't completely right yet, he stayed in his room most of the day. In the afternoon his father and Georgia went over to the Gibbses', but no one pressed Stewart to go.

"Tell Ozgood hello for me," Stewart called from the top of the stairs just before they went out. "Or Froggy, whichever he happens to be," he added when the door was closed.

He hadn't wanted to check on bus schedules with his father in the house. There was always the danger that he would pick up one of the other phones and accidentally overhear something. Now he looked up the number and with a shaking hand, he dialed. An elderly sounding woman answered. She answered his question with, "Bus travel isn't so popular nowadays. There's only one bus to Tulsa, kiddo. Leaves here every day at five thirty sharp. You planning a trip to Tulsa, are you?"

"Maybe, thank you." He hung up the phone and groaned. The woman sounded nosy. She'd want to know why he was going, and she would be sure to remember him if anyone came in to ask. The bus would leave right around the middle of the basketball game. Dad would be at the game. He always sat on the home side of the gym. Because of the way the bleachers are built up, he couldn't have a good view of the bench on our side. Stewart would play badly and be put on the bench. He could leave, and Dad wouldn't know he was gone until the game was over. By that time the bus would have arrived in Tulsa, and he would just have to disappear. But where would he go? And what about the bus station woman? He would have to have a disguise. He called Rachel.

The next day at school there was no hope for getting his mind on anything except the plan, and he was pretty sure Rachel and Ham had the same problem. They talked before school, between classes, and at lunch. Rachel and Ham were already at the table when he got through the line. Heading toward them and dropping his tray there, he could feel Taylor's eyes on him. He did not look up at her, but he had hardly started on his spaghetti when he heard her voice. "What's the deal, Stewart?" she asked. "I mean why are you sitting with . . . ," she paused for a minute then went on, "these two?"

"They are my friends, Taylor." He didn't want to hurt her feelings. "You're real cool and everything, but Rachel and Ham have been my friends for a long time. This is where I belong."

For just a minute she stared at him, her eyes big with wonder. "You *are* weird. I mean, totally weird. Well, good-bye, Wart." He did not watch her move away, wasn't even tempted to watch her behind in movement.

When game time came, Stewart was ready. He had taken the cologne bottle from his locker and dropped it in the hallway trashcan. Rachel, who had made it to the thrift shop just before closing, had supplied him with the disguise he had stored in his gym bag.

"You didn't show me a whole lot in practice today," Coach told Stewart, "but I'm starting you anyway."

He played hard, running and jumping with all the strength he had. Once he intercepted a pass, drove the ball down the court, weaving through his opponents and made the layup. You did that, he told himself, you, not witchcraft. It felt good to hear the crowd cheer, knowing he truly deserved it. The next time he got the ball he fumbled and had it taken away from him. A few minutes later, the boy he was guarding made a shot he should have stopped. He wasn't surprised when a substitute came to slap his hand.

He did not mind sitting on the bench. He was certain his playing truly had improved since the beginning of the season. He'd continue to practice hard and be even better by next year.

By the beginning of the second quarter, he was ready to make his move. He'd rely on his old standby. "My stomach feels funny," he told the coach. "I might throw up." Stewart knew that was a threat that got a kid excused from anything.

"Go to the locker room," the coach said, and he did. When he came out, he looked like a little old lady in a faded long dress and a big hat, pulled down to hide part of his face. Walking all bent over, he was pretty proud of his disguise until he noticed his high tops sticking out beneath the hem of his skirt. Oh, well, it was the best he could do. Besides lots of people wear athletic shoes. Maybe this old lady is a jogger.

He moved along keeping his head down, and he thought things were going well. He had to go through the concession area, though, and there he froze for a second. His father stood at the counter, only a couple of feet away. Stewart heard him order popcorn, then the man behind him said, "Your boy in the game?"

"Not right now," his father answered. You're wrong,

Dad, Stewart thought. I'm in the game all right. I'm in a really big game, and I have to play well. Finally, he had the nerve to ease his body along the concession wall. The exit was on the other side, and he leaned, ever so slightly, and looked around the corner. The coast was clear, so the little old lady jogger lifted her skirt up to her hairy knees, and she ran, her blue and white high tops moving with great speed.

The cool air hit his face, and he took in a big breath. He could see the taxi. Thanks, Rach, he thought. She had watched for him to leave the bench, had called a taxi on her cell, and it pulled up just as he burst out the gym door. "The bus station," Stewart said, trying to use his high voice. "I've got to make the bus to Tulsa. My daughter, no she's my granddaughter, is having a baby, twins, two babies."

The driver turned around in his seat to look at him. "Lady . . . ," he paused. Stewart's heart pounded hard in his ears. "Lady, are you sure you're okay? You sound kind of sick."

"Please, just hurry, sonny," Stewart squeaked. The driver shrugged, then turned back in his seat and eased the taxi into the street.

At the station Stewart handed the driver the fare, pulled up his skirt, and jumped out. When Stewart looked back, the driver was sitting there watching him and shaking his head. Because the woman had said bus travel was down, he was surprised to see the station fairly full. He stood for a while near the door, working up his nerve to approach the ticket box. He had hoped for a different person, but the woman behind the counter was as old as Gran.

He pulled down his hat and hobbled toward her. "One ticket for Tulsa." He made his voice high and kept his head down.

"Round trip?"

"No, one way."

"Staying awhile, are you?"

"Going home." He pushed a twenty-dollar bill toward her and wished she would just give him the ticket.

"Good thing you got here when you did. Bus going to be fairly full of people going on to Tulsa when it gets here, not too many tickets left. Things pick up around the holidays."

"Umm," Stewart grunted. He took the ticket and his change and turned away. There was a spot to sit near the door, and he moved toward it, remembering to bend his back and hobble along. On the bench, he looked up to see the ticket woman staring at him. Any minute she could figure out something was fishy and call the police. He had noticed a patrol car parked on the street when he got out of the taxi.

For just a minute he squirmed, but then he made a wonderful discovery right beside him. Someone had left a newspaper. He grabbed it up and unfolded it in front of his face. It took a second to realize he held it upside down, but he flipped it quickly.

Before long the lady announced the arrival of the bus, but she also said that before new passengers could board, the current passengers would be allowed to get off for ten minutes if they wanted to. Those people would have a chance to get back on first. Stewart watched as they came into the station. One young woman had two little kids with her and a baby in her arms. She struggled, trying to get inside. Stewart felt tempted to get up to help, but he was afraid of getting that close to anyone and of drawing attention to himself. Finally, a man from behind her stepped up to hold the door.

Stewart's watch was in his gym bag, along with the clothes he had worn to school. Under his dress, he still wore his basketball uniform. Looking over the newspaper, he could see that the big clock on the wall said 5:20. He waited what seemed like a long time, then looked back. The minute hand hadn't even moved. He wanted out of the bus station. Should he go outside to wait? No, it was pretty cold. His coat was in the bag, but of course it didn't look like an old lady's coat. Someone might see him shivering and take pity on an elderly lady. He couldn't risk getting anyone else involved. He tried to read an article about the animal shelter's campaign to find homes for dogs and cats.

After what seemed like forever, the woman announced that new passengers bound for Tulsa could now board the bus. Stewart got in line, grateful that the late-autumn light was growing dim. The driver stopped taking tickets and leaned around the two people in front of Stewart. Was he going to ask questions? Stewart held his breath. "Let me take your bag, ma'am," the man said to him.

"Thank you," Stewart said in his high voice, and then he was climbing the steps. The bus was fairly crowded, but Stewart was relieved to see a spot with two empty seats. He dropped into the one by the window, hoping no one would sit with him. Just before they took off, an elderly woman got on. Stewart knew she would sit beside him, and she did. Well, he said to himself, at least old ladies are nice, but then as she settled herself, he remembered he was one too. She'll want to socialize, he thought, and sure enough she did. "Do you knit?" she asked, and she dug into a small bag.

"Not anymore," Stewart muttered. "My machine is broken."

"Machine?" The woman pulled something that looked like a sweater out of the bag. "I said knit, dear."

"Knit! Oh, knit! How silly of me. I thought you said fit, you know, like fit dresses." Stewart looked around for another seat and tried to think of an excuse to move. It didn't matter. There were no more empty seats.

"I've got an extra sweater with me, if you want something to pass the time," the woman said.

"That's lovely," Stewart said in his high voice. "But the light is so dim, and my eyes aren't so good since my last hospital stay."

"Hospital, oh, my dear, you've been sick, too, have

you? Well, I'll tell you about my hospital stay. It'll make you feel lucky."

She told him and told him and told him, all about her gall bladder, her indigestion, and her hernia. At least Stewart wasn't called on to say much except, "Really," and "You poor thing." Still, even with just those few words his old lady voice was making his throat really tired. "You'll have to excuse me," he said after a while. "I simply must nap." He turned his head to rest on the window, then shut his eyes. The sound of the tires on the highway suddenly seemed loud to him. This bus was taking him into a city, a place where he did not know his way around. In his wallet, he had around fifty dollars, all the money the three of them had been able to come up with. He had even taken ten dollars from Georgia's bank, replacing it with a note that promised repayment.

Once in Tulsa, he would make his way to the YWCA. It had been Rachel's idea, and she had checked on the price of rooms there. He'd have to stay in his old lady clothes, but it was the only place he could stay cheaply enough. He couldn't go to the men's Y as himself, and his dad might hold out for a couple of days. He'd get himself a supply of cheap food and stay in his room, waiting. He'd been smart enough to bring a couple of books he'd been wanting to read.

Stewart felt a touch on his arm. "We're coming to the station, dear. You might want to wake up."

It took him a second to find his high voice, so he moved his head and shoulders from side to side as if he were stiff before he said, "Oh yes, thank you."

"Nice visiting with you," said his seatmate before she stood up to get off, and he grunted. It was around seven, and the world Stewart saw as he stepped down from the bus was dark and unfamiliar, but what he heard was familiar, horrifyingly familiar.

"Stewart, oh, Stewart, over here." He whirled to his left, and there she was! Wanda Gibbs was just a few feet from him.

Run, he thought, but his feet didn't work. He felt drained and beaten. She moved to stand beside him, reached for his arm, and got a firm hold. "I'm so glad I found you, darling," she said. "I'll bet you're starved. There's a little restaurant next door," she said. "Let's get something to eat."

"How could . . ." He was going to say how could you get here so soon, but the question died in his throat. He knew how she could get there so fast. She's a witch, remember? Suddenly he felt drained. His entire body slumped. There was no fighting Wanda Gibbs. He might as well give up.

Stewart thought she must be able to see that he was beaten because she let go of his arm. She smiled at him. "Wouldn't you like to go inside and put on your own clothes first? I'll wait out here."

He stumbled through the station entrance and found

the men's room. "You've got the wrong door, ma'am," said a big man who was coming out, but Stewart ignored him, went on in, took off the dress and the basketball uniform beneath it. As if in a dream, he moved to put on his jeans, shirt, and jacket from his gym bag. He threw the dress and hat into the trash can. His old lady days were over, so were his days as a happy kid. He was about to become the stepson of a witch. There was nothing, not one thing, he could do about it.

Outside, Ms. Gibbs waited for him. She waved when he came out the door. Stewart didn't feel upset, not really, just incredibly tired, like he'd been walked on all over. They did not speak, just moved through the night to the building next door and found a booth. Ms. Gibbs ordered them both hamburgers. "I was pretty sure you'd head to Tulsa," she said with no explanation as to how she had gotten there so fast. Your father is out searching the streets at home. We agreed to check with Martha every two hours. I'll call her after a bit."

After a reasonable amount of time, Stewart thought, and then he let his mind go blank. He hadn't said a word, and he had no intention of doing so. Ms. Gibbs didn't press him to talk until just before the food came, so when she said, "What is it, Stewart, that makes you so determined to keep your father from marrying me?"

He looked into those deep green eyes. Well, he was beaten anyway. He might as well lay his cards on the table. "I know you're a witch," he said more calmly than he'd imagined possible. "You're a witch, and I don't like what you are doing to Georgia or my father."

His head was down now, and he waited. Would she turn him into a frog right there, walk out, and tell his dad she hadn't seen him? It was the laugh that made him look up.

"Stewart," she said, still smiling, "if I can do anything unusual, it is because I use my mind, all of it. Most people only use about 10 percent of their mental ability, did you know that? For instance, I was able to sense right away that you had left the gymnasium." She laughed again. "A witch! Your imagination is as active as Ozgood's." She shook her head. "I'm not so sure I'm up to being a mother to you and him both, even though Georgia is responding well to my attentions."

He looked into her eyes again. "I won't be easy to live with, not when I get my strength back. I'm warning you. I'll . . ." He searched for a word. "I'll be Wart," he said. "That's what they called King Arthur, you know, when he was young. I'll be the worst Wart you've ever seen."

She laughed again. "You know," she said, "it would have been easier for you if your dad had married Martha long ago."

"I know," he said. "Boy am I sorry he didn't."

She took a cell phone from her purse. "Finish your burger. I'll call Martha and tell her I found you." She slid out of the booth and moved a few feet away.

In her car he fell asleep. After what seemed like a very

short time, they were stopping in front of his house. His father's car was there, and so was Martha's. He thought Ms. Gibbs would get out and come in with him. She didn't, and she didn't even say good-bye.

Martha was in there waiting with his father. Her face was all red, and Stewart could see that she'd been crying. He was afraid of what his dad would say, but instead of saying anything, he only hugged Stewart. Then Martha hugged him too. Good old comfortable Martha. Her hug made Stewart remember what it had been like way back when he had a mother.

"Go on up and hit the sack," his dad said. "We'll talk in the morning."

Stewart was still exhausted, but sleep didn't come again right away. After quite a while he started to wonder if his father was asleep. He got up and looked in his dad's room. He wasn't there. He started down the stairs, but the sound of voices made him stop. Ms. Gibbs, he thought, she's come back. When he got closer, though, he could tell it wasn't Wanda Gibbs his father was talking to. It was Martha. Why would Martha be there so late? He considered sneaking down to listen, but suddenly he was too tired to even go down the stairs. He stumbled his way back to bed.

The smell of bacon and eggs and the sound of his dad singing "Jingle Bells" greeted Stewart as he came down to the kitchen in the morning. "I let you sleep late, called your school, and told them you'd be there late. I don't have a class this morning, and . . . ," he hesitated, "you and I have got to talk." His father held a plate out to him.

"Can I eat first?" Stewart moved over to look into the skillet. "I sort of lose my appetite when I get yelled at." His father laughed. That's a good sign, Stewart thought. He loaded his plate and sat down.

"I'm not going to yell at you." His father came over to sit across from him. Stewart did not quit eating, but he looked up, very interested. "I'm not even going to try to explain anything to you because I can't explain anything to myself."

"What?" Stewart said around a mouthful of food. He swallowed and went on. "What can't you explain?"

Dad put both hands around his coffee cup and sort of rubbed it between them. "Something happened to me last night." He set the cup down and drew a deep breath. "I don't know. Right in the middle of worrying about you I started to wonder what I was doing dating Wanda Gibbs." He picked up the cup and started the rolling motion again.

"You mean because of my note, because I said I couldn't accept her?" Stewart said.

Dad shook his head slowly. "No, that's the strange part. It wasn't just you. It was . . ." He put down the cup and rubbed the sides of his head. "I can't explain it. I'm not a man who just changes how he feels, but suddenly I did not like the idea of marrying Wanda Gibbs. I didn't even like the idea of dating her. Sounds crazy, doesn't it?" He shook his head. "It's like I stepped out of a fog or something."

Stewart opened his mouth to say spell. He wanted to say that his father had been under a spell, but he didn't. Things were going his way. His sensible college-professor dad would never believe the witch story, and anyway there was no explanation for why the spell had been suddenly broken. "So you won't be seeing Ms. Gibbs anymore?"

"Not in a romantic way. I suppose I'll see her, you know. She's a good friend of Martha's."

"Yeah, Martha. What about Martha? Are you going to start taking her out again?"

"I hope so. We talked last night. Neither of us wants to rush into anything."

Stewart got up to fill his plate again. "I like Martha a lot, Dad. Thinking you might marry Ms. Gibbs sure made me change my mind about having Martha for a stepmother."

"I know." Dad stood up. "Now, I've got to do something hard. I've got to go over to Wanda's and tell her our relationship won't go any further. Go upstairs and get dressed as soon as you're finished. I'll drop you off on my way to Wanda's."

At school, he went by the art room on his way to check in at the office. Mr. Harrison was in there smiling as he passed out paints. He had a little Christmas decoration in his beard, but for Mr. Harrison that wasn't crazy. Stewart waved when Mr. Harrison looked up.

He told Rachel and Ham his news at lunch. She clapped and Ham made hooting noises until the teacher on cafeteria duty moved in their direction. It was Rachel who brought up Ozgood. "I know we don't want to be around Ms. Gibbs, but what about that little boy? I feel sorry for him."

Stewart shrugged. "Yeah, I was getting attached to Ozgood too. Maybe after some time goes by, it would be safe to ask about spending some time with him. I'll ask Martha."

But there was never a chance for Stewart to spend time with Ozgood. The Gibbs family was gone. His father told him that evening when he first came home. "I was shocked. There was just a note on the door. She said our relationship was a mistake. Ended the message with, 'Ozgood and I will find happiness elsewhere.' The woman is full of surprises."

"Really?" Stewart watched his father take off his coat and hang it in the hall closet. "You aren't sorry, are you?"

Dad let out a long slow breath. "Relieved is more like it." He laughed. "There I was worrying about breaking up with her when she had already dumped me." He closed the closet door. "Come on, let's see what Gran left for dinner."

That evening, Stewart felt more relaxed than he had felt for a very long time. He felt good, in fact, all that week. On Saturday morning, he took Ozgood's rabbit picture to a frame shop and was pleased to learn he could pick it up that afternoon. The frame was expensive, but he had enough savings left for Christmas gifts.

He bought Ham enough candy and junk food to fill a great big box. He got a nice silver frame for Martha and hoped she would be putting a wedding picture in it soon. For his father he picked out a nice pen set and puppy toys for Georgia, who was now the proud owner of the last little Dot. It was Rachel's gift, though, that pleased him most. He saw it in a jewelry store, a necklace with a small sterling silver frog. The man inside attached a small metal plate on the front, and Stewart asked him to engrave the word *thanks* on it.

When, finally, he made his way home with all his purchases, he was surprised and pleased to see Martha's car parked in the driveway.

"Hi, everybody," he called when he came in, but only Martha answered him. She was putting spaghetti in a pot of boiling water.

"Where's Dad?" he asked.

Martha leaned her head toward the backyard. "He and Georgia took the little Dot outside, starting housebreaking, you know."

Stewart set his packages on the table. "I like having you here," he said, and she smiled at him. He pulled Ozgood's picture from a bag. "Doesn't this look great?"

"Oh, it does!" She turned from the stove to touch the

frame. "He gave me a rabbit picture too. I think I'll also get mine framed."

A thought flashed through Stewart's mind. "You know, the evening Ozgood drew this he was here, and he told me that he and his mother moved here as a favor to you."

Martha looked at him for a long time. "He told you that?" She turned back to the stove.

Stewart put the picture back into the bag, put the bag on the table, and waited. When it was clear that she intended to say nothing more, he moved over to stand so that he could see her face. "Is that true? Did they come here as a favor to you?"

"Stew," Martha said, and she smiled at him. "I don't expect you to tell me everything. Do you think maybe you could show me the same courtesy?"

Stewart didn't know what to say, but just then his father and Georgia came in the back door with little Dot. "He did it," Georgia sang out. "Little Dot is about to get his potty trained."

"Are you going to give that puppy a name?" asked Martha. "You know you and Stewart wouldn't want to be called just 'little Wrights.'"

Stewart tried hard to get his mind on puppy names. He did not want to think about what Martha had just said. "You could call him Spot," he suggested.

What Happened Last

It was a long time, well after Christmas, before Stewart told anyone about that conversation with Martha. He finally told Rachel and Ham in January, but before that happened some other things happened.

For one thing, Stewart and his family didn't go to California during Christmas vacation to see Sammi and her parents. They went instead with Martha to visit her mother and father in Hawaii, where they had retired. Stewart and Georgia had a great time on the beaches, and Martha's parents made them feel like family.

Sammi, though, was disappointed. She sent him an e-mail while he was in Hawaii. "Poor Stewart, dragged off to Hawaii by his wicked stepmother-to-be! Breaks my heart! Wow! Maybe next time your cousin will get invited too. How are Rachel and Ham?"

Stewart had lots to tell Rachel and Ham about the

trip. They were sitting in the sunroom watching Georgia and Spot playing in the backyard. After Stewart had talked what for him was a long time, he blurted out the story of his talk with Martha. "I just can't seem to forget that Ms. Gibbs moved here to do Martha a favor." He got up from his place on the wicker chair and began to pace. "I mean the woman might be a real witch. Why would Martha need her to move here?"

"Beats me," said Ham. Rachel didn't say anything, just turned her head away.

"What?" said Stewart. "Come on, Rach. You've got an idea. Don't you?"

"You know, Stew." She turned back to face him. "Or at least you would if you thought about the whole thing logically."

"Tell me," he said.

She sighed. "Martha always wanted to marry your father, but you didn't want a stepmother, right?" Stewart nodded, and she went on. "So Martha calls in her friendly witch friend, who puts big-time moves on your dad. He falls under her spell." She shrugged and held her hands out, palms up. "Compared to Wanda Witch, Martha suddenly seems to you like the best thing that could happen to your dad." She snapped her fingers, "And poof, Wanda disappears just in time for your dad and Martha to get married."

"But they aren't married," Stewart said.

"They will be. We all know that, and we all know

your dad would never have married her or anyone else you couldn't accept. I don't think even Ms. Gibbs and her spell could have actually pulled that off."

Stewart slumped back into his chair, dropping his head to rest his face in his hands. Ham reached out to put a hand on his shoulder.

"We don't have to talk about it, Stew," said Rachel. "You don't even have to think about it. Just let the whole thing go."

"Go," said Ham. "That's a great idea! Let's go to the movies. School starts back tomorrow."

At the theater, Rachel and Ham discussed which of the three movies they should see. Stewart stared, unseeing, at the movie poster in front of him. "Doesn't matter to me," he said, and he thought about the seating arrangement. Sometimes lately he had felt something strange, almost uncomfortable, when he was close to Rachel. Ham and Rachel settled on a movie that was supposed to be funny. Stewart hung back silently, behind them. Inside, Rachel chose an empty row of seats and started in. She would go to the center, where she liked to sit. Ham was next in line, but he stepped aside and motioned for Stewart to follow Rachel. Stewart shrugged and went in. Well, the movie was a comedy, so being beside Rachel would be fun. They always laughed at the same things.

Stewart slid down in the seat and held the popcorn so that both Ham and Rachel could reach it. The movie was funny, lots of good lines. During a comic car race, Stewart and Rachel both moved forward as they laughed. Their bodies met at the armrest, and an almost electric sensation shot through Stewart. Suddenly neither of them was laughing. They were looking at each other, and Stewart knew. He knew that Rachel felt the electricity, too, and he knew something he had not known before. Now he knew it was okay. His relationship with Rachel was changing, and that was okay. He felt no pressure, no need to consult Sammi for advice, no need to make any declarations, at least not yet. For right now, just knowing was enough. There was, though, one question he needed to ask.

Ham's sister picked them up after the movie. She stopped the car in front of Rachel's house and Rachel got out, yelling back her good-byes. Stewart put his hand on the door, but he didn't open it immediately. "Hey," he said to Ham, "I got to ask you something. Back there at the movie, why'd you make me sit next to Rachel?"

Ham laughed. "You got to ask? Man, don't you know anything? Rach is crazy about you. It's been that way a long time."

Stewart waved dismissively. "I thought you might have some wild idea like that. You're nuts!" He got out of the car and smiled all the way into the house and up to his room.

Rachel was right about the marriage. It happened in the spring. Stewart's father asked him to be the best man. Georgia was the junior bridesmaid, wearing the pink dress Ms. Gibbs had made for her. Martha had never been married before, and she wanted a formal ceremony with lots of guests.

It was a beautiful wedding, and it would have been perfect if only Stewart had been just slightly less observant. He was standing beside his father watching Martha as she came in to walk down the aisle. It was just an instant that she turned to the right and smiled. Stewart looked to her right too. The only light came from candles that produced shadows. He almost didn't see them standing in the doorway. He almost missed Ozgood and Ms. Gibbs, her fingers forming the victory sign. Steady, he told himself. It would not look good if the best man fainted at the altar.